Angel in Vegas

Angel in Vegas

THE CHRONICLES OF NOAH SARK

Norma Howe

CANDLEWICK PRESS

F
How

5/11

Text copyright © 2009 by Norma Howe
Doodle artwork copyright © 2009 by Ted Howe

Hound Dog
Words and Music by Jerry Leiber and Mike Stoller
Copyright © 1956 Elvis Presley Music, Inc. and Lion Publishing Co., Inc.
Copyright renewed, Assigned to Gladys Music and Universal Music Corp.
All rights administered by Cherry Lane Music Publishing Company, Inc.
International Copyright Secured
All Rights Reserved

First edition 2009

Library of Congress Cataloging-in-Publication Data

Howe, Norma.
Angel in Vegas : the chronicles of Noah Sark / Norma Howe. — 1st ed.
p.   cm.
Summary: A demoted guardian angel whose previous "assignment" was Princess Diana now finds himself enjoying the oddball diversions of Las Vegas in the body of a teenage boy, with a teenage girl as his newest charge.
ISBN 978-0-7636-3985-3
[1. Guardian angels—Fiction. 2. Angels—Fiction.
3. Friendship—Fiction. 4. Las Vegas (Nev.)—Fiction.]   I. Title.
PZ7.H8376An 2009
[Fic]—dc22   2008028758

09 10 11 12 13 14 BVG 10 9 8 7 6 5 4 3 2 1

Printed in Berryville, VA, U.S.A.

This book was typeset in Filosofia.

Candlewick Press
99 Dover Street
Somerville, Massachusetts 02144

visit us at www.candlewick.com

For Angel Jake, my eternal
Best Buddy, and for
mon cher ami Margaret.
(Vers la droite! Vers la droite!)

But most of all for Barbra and Andy.
You guys were FANTABULOUS—and
I'll try my darndest never to forget you.

Noah

CHAPTER ONE

IT WAS HARD, the way I had to leave them — Andy and The Girl, I mean — by sneaking off like I did without even telling them that this was really good-bye. But I had to. My job was over and I had to go. What made it even harder was realizing that I had actually fallen for The Girl in a big way. I'm sure she knew it, and I know she liked me, too — but exactly how much, I wasn't quite sure. As for her and Andy, well, in the beginning I thought that he just wasn't cut out for long-term commitments and they had already been together for over three weeks, about two weeks past his limit, according to the way I had it figured. But now, you know, I think there may be some hope for the two of them after all — especially after today, with me no longer in the picture, waiting patiently for her to finally take note of my irresistible charms and fall insanely in love with me.

It was Andy who suggested that we stop for a bite to eat at this popular little deli place on Main Street in Angels Camp, a little town in the California Gold Country, and while we were waiting for our food, I was still trying to puzzle out if it was *really* time for me to leave, even though I knew it was. It's funny, isn't it, how when you don't want to do something but know you should, you make up all kinds of excuses for not doing it? But this wasn't some simple personal thing, like ignoring the THANK YOU hint at the fast-food place and just leaving your messy tray and sloppy containers on the table for someone else to clean up, telling yourself that it really wasn't *your* job to be an unpaid busboy. No, this was serious business, and the little extra push I needed appeared (of all places) on the *Noon News* that was airing on the little TV set stuck up on the wall behind the cash register at the deli. It all flashed by so fast that even Andy and The Girl didn't notice, but it was clear to me that it was just *too* coincidental to be *merely* a coincidence. No, it was an unmistakable message aimed solely and directly at me from those powerful forces Up Above whose will I dare not question. The writing was on the television. It was as simple as that.

My big problem was how I was going to make my getaway. I just couldn't walk out of the deli as free as the breeze with both of them sitting there so close to the door. After thinking about it for a few minutes, I got an idea. I'd quietly excuse myself to go to the john, and then I'd jump out of the window and take off, even if I did have to leave my rucksack behind. But wouldn't you know it, there was no window in there — just the deli's maintenance man doing some minor repairs and distracting me with his chatter. So much for *that* brilliant scheme. Back at our table, I toyed briefly with the idea of using the old hummingbird trick on them — you know, where you point behind their backs and exclaim, "Hummingbird!" and when they turn around to look for it, you quickly disappear around a corner. But while that ploy sometimes works with little children, it was way too absurd in my current situation, and I had to admonish myself to really put my mind to this and *get serious*.

But then, after a short spell, I had another idea, except this time it was really original and downright earthshaking. "Hey, guys," I said. "I'm going next door to get a pack of cigarettes. Be back in a minute." I grabbed my rucksack and nonchalantly slung it over my shoulder.

The Girl quickly reached over and caught my arm. "You can leave that here," she said. "We'll watch it."

Our eyes met briefly. "Nah — that's okay. I've got it."

Andy had been pretty quiet up until then, just looking around the room and gently pounding his fists together, the way people do sometimes when they're nervous or impatient, waiting for something to happen. But now he suddenly raised his hand and pointed his finger at me. "Wait," he said. "I thought you told me last night that you were going to *quit* smoking."

"Well, I am." I forced a grin. "Tomorrow."

"That's just great," he muttered, and then did that little thing where he managed to scratch his ear and adjust his eyeglasses all in one coordinated move. I'm really going to miss that.

About The Girl, though, I just couldn't leave without touching her one last time. Not that I had touched her all that much up to then. To tell the truth, I had hardly touched her at all — in a meaningful way, that is — except for last night in my dream, but that was something completely different. I thought that I deserved at least one special moment all for myself, just to remember her by.

"Oops, your collar's turned under," I said, even though it wasn't. Summoning forth all the human courage I could muster, I began to fumble awkwardly with the neckline of her leopard-print blouse. The side of her neck felt smooth and slightly damp to my touch, and time stood still for about a thousand years.

Finally, she reached up herself to check on my progress, and our fingers briefly touched on that magical curvature of skin hidden beneath a silky sheaf of her wheat-blonde hair.

"*Merci*," she said simply, her little smile turning my poor heart to mush. At that moment I had to literally pinch my lips together with my fingers to keep from blurting out the truth to her. Oh, how I longed to kneel at her feet and confess my secret — to let her know that there was much, *much* more to me than she could ever imagine.

But I didn't weaken. I didn't waver. I started to walk away, resolute, but after taking a few steps, I couldn't help turning back to gaze upon her one last time. "*Adieu!*" I raised my hand in an overly dramatic farewell gesture. "*Adieu, adieu —*"

Andy suddenly made a funny snorting noise, breaking the spell. He was annoyed by the way The Girl and I had begun mixing French words and phrases into our conversation the night before in Las Vegas, and even more once we were in his uncle Buck's new Cessna 182, flying out of Vegas early this morning. But how could she know that I really wasn't joking? How could she know that this really was good-bye? As far as she and Andy were concerned, I was only going next door to get a pack of cigarettes.

"*Adieu,*" she answered back, blowing me an exaggerated kiss. She followed that with downcast eyes, a hopeless shrug, and a murmured, "*C'est la guerre.*"

It's the war didn't make any sense right then, but it was one of her favorite expressions. "*Toujours, c'est la guerre,*" she repeated, even more dramatically, and I was suddenly caught in that no-man's-land somewhere between laughter and tears. I turned away quickly, alarmed at the rush of emotion that almost took my breath away, for I had yet to master the studied ability of teenage boys to control the sudden onset of unexpected tears.

"Better hurry back," Andy called after me, half rising from his chair. "Our burgers will be here in a minute."

"Don't worry." I swallowed quickly, turning to face him. "I'll be back in a flash."

"Wait," he said, suddenly standing up and pushing his chair to one side. "I'll go with you."

The Girl reached out and pulled on his shirt. "Oh, sit down, Andy. He doesn't need you tagging along. Jeez." My spirits sagged at the harshness of her tone, but then she followed up with a few words that lifted them right back up again; she touched his arm, and when their eyes met, she added in a soft and gentle tone, almost like an apology, "Really, he doesn't."

Andy finally sat down again, but hesitantly. Then he looked at his watch, twisting it around and around on his wrist. "Just hurry back," he said.

Anyway, long story short, now I'm safely aboard the Greyhound, heading back to Vegas and wondering how I might sneak a cigarette. Ah, the cigarette! Therein lies the solution to the little mystery that had been bothering me ever since I arrived in Las Vegas yesterday morning — or *appeared*, if you want to be more specific. And the mystery is this: what is the purpose of my being addicted to cigarettes, when I'm only sixteen and teenage smoking is not cool anymore? But now the reason had become clear: it had afforded me with a perfect alibi for my getaway! I mean, my new friends would have been really suspicious if I'd gone off to buy cigarettes when I didn't even smoke, right?

It's hard to believe that after night falls on earth, I shall be reunited with my special band of companions at that glorious place where night *never* falls and where my colleagues are eagerly awaiting my safe return with that self-assured confidence that is an integral part of our blessed and eternal nature. Yes, it's true. Guardian Angels *are* blessed, and they *are* eternal, and I am privileged to count myself among their number.

Okay, hold on. Just hold on a moment, okay? It was bound to come out sooner or later, and I've decided that it is neither good nor fair to keep you in the dark until I earn a modicum of your trust and then suddenly hit you with it — like *bam!* So please, don't get excited and go all crazy on me, especially if you happen to be that one American out of four who actually has a *problem* with Angels. If that's you — if you fit that description — I want to extend a very special invitation to you to just stand by me for a while and at least hear me out while I relate to you everything that I know about my latest adventure — or, to put it more accurately, my latest *assignment,* which began yesterday morning and is quickly drawing to a close.

Of course, there is always the possibility that I may be waylaid somewhere along the route back to Vegas, but I'm trusting completely in my special blessed status to outwit any Devilish attempts to thwart the successful completion of my mission.

I adjust my seat and gaze out the window. There's not much to see, so I find myself reliving the memories of these past two days and the glorious times I've had with Barbra and Andy. After a while I get the urge to indulge in one of my favorite ways of whiling away the time Up Above when eternity starts to drag — and that is the fine art known as doodling. So I root around in my rucksack until I locate my extra-fine-point ReadyEver pencil and my daily planner notebook and set to work making my memories come alive. I must admit, however, that while I'm a regular Michelangelo Up Above, I'm always somewhat disappointed to see how the quality of my little doodles invariably takes a nosedive once I arrive on earth. (Although, judging by your ordinary standards, I've seen a lot worse.)

Now, at this moment, as I'm finally drifting off into a fitful sleep, I see again in my mind's eye the final segment of the *Noon News* that was airing at the deli in

Angels Camp. There is the reporter, announcing that she is broadcasting from Angelo's Donut Emporium in Las Vegas, Nevada — the very same place where I first found myself early yesterday morning. She is interviewing Angelo himself and relating how the catch phrase "Ka-*Boom*sy!" somehow set off the wild and crazy fracas that had just taken place in the shop. I'll tell you more about that later when I come to it, but as for me, my destiny was set at the precise moment that the TV camera — panning around the shop — paused for just a split second on the pure white stool that was situated in back of the counter and adjacent to the cold-drinks refrigerator case. Yes, *that* stool, standing there in all its mystical glory, beckoning to me, calling me home. *The way back home, the way back home, is right before my eyes.*

But now I must strive to overcome this longing ache in my heart that keeps urging me to remain in your strange and wonderful place — a place (I should explain) dubbed WackiWorld by my friend and colleague Angel Jake, based on his observation that some of the things you people believe "just don't make a lick of sense." But be that as it may, I have to go back. There is no other way. As much as it pains me, I must return to Paradise.

CHAPTER TWO

THE FIRST FEW MOMENTS ON THE JOB of a new and special task are always confusing for us Guardian Angels, and this assignment was no different for me. I had no idea where I was in relation to the rest of your world just yesterday morning when I suddenly found myself standing on a white and black tile floor, about to enter the men's room in what appeared to be a coffee shop or sit-down bakery.

At first I feared that I was back in Paris, destined to relive the shock and horror of that awful August night in '97, with the beloved Princess Diana lying crushed and mortally wounded in the tangled wreckage, all because of my own selfish ineptness and utter stupidity. Even if it wasn't possible for me to be right there in the car with her that fateful night, I foolishly and tragically failed to place her under those special powers that we Guardian Angels have come to refer to as Protective Surveillance.

Remember your first romantic crush, and how it was nigh impossible to entertain thoughts of anything other than your beloved for more than a few seconds at a time? Well, that is exactly what we Angels must do in order to keep our powers of Protective Surveillance in force on those occasions when we are not able to be in direct contact with our earthly charges. It sounds simple enough, but I must confess that I fell victim to the one deadly pitfall that has plagued us Angels forever — the insidious trap called Distraction. In short, while the Princess was in mortal danger, my mind was otherwise occupied — to put it in the most innocent and least self-accusatory terms I can think of.

After numberless assignments down through the ages, this deal with the British Princess had been my first experience with failure, and it was truly, *truly* devastating. Furthermore, I was totally unprepared for the shock I was to experience upon my return to my Heavenly Abode. Instead of the traditional rejoicing with my companions of the spirit, I was whisked away to a special section reserved for the humbled and humiliated, where I was soon surrounded by countless numbers of my fellow failures, all with their own sorry excuses of Deadly Distraction just when their Angelic help was most desperately needed by the unfortunate human beings under their care.

Oh, I can't even count the number of times that I have wanted to kick myself for my unforgivably selfish blunder that night, a mistake so embarrassing that I can hardly bear to *think* about it, let alone confess it to you now. But every time I start to figure out exactly how I can give myself a good swift kick, I'm reminded by my Angelic superiors that although violence is a basic necessity on earth, it is strictly forbidden in Heaven, even if it *is* both self-inflicted and justly deserved.

But there I go again — shamelessly trivializing my monumental error by suggesting that it could be atoned for by a simple self-administered kick! Alas, it is not that easy. I see now that I must continue to repent and try to make amends not merely *forever* but forever *and ever.*

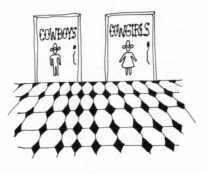

CHAPTER THREE

THINKING ABOUT THE PRINCESS while standing there at the entrance to the men's room sent me once again into a maelstrom of self-incrimination and guilt. *Oh, will I ever be able to breathe freely again? Is there anything worse than the regret and guilt of a GA who has failed his sacred duty to preserve and protect the precious life of the one person entrusted to his care? Oh, such misery! Oh, such woe! Oh, such bitter Paris memories! But wait! What is this I see before me? The letters on the door through which I'm about to enter spell out the word* COWBOYS, *and right next to it, another door proclaims* COWGIRLS. *So I am not in France after all! Cowboys? Cowgirls? Is it possible that I am in America?*

And then the truth suddenly struck me like a lightning bolt from Heaven, although I hasten to report that we never have lightning there, or bad weather of any kind. But by the sudden onset of the unmistakable warning cramp on the left side of my head, I instantly knew that the message I was about to receive was reliable and true.

Unlikely as it sounds, and unworthy as I am, I seemed to have been blessed with the rare opportunity of a second chance. It was suddenly made clear to me that by performing my newly assigned duties with precision and care, I might earn the right to redeem myself for my sorry performance on that sad and somber night in Paris. If I successfully completed my upcoming mission, I would soon be able to rejoin my regular Heavenly companions with my head held high — spiritually speaking, of course, since we don't actually *have* heads in Heaven. Except when we're singing, that is, which we do a lot of. What I mean to say is that we *do* have heads then, when we're singing, but *peculiar* heads — that is, they're not exactly what *you* would call heads, since we are primarily spiritual beings. They're actually — oh, never mind. It's just too hard to explain. I don't mean to be rude, but you wouldn't be able to process it anyway. You'll understand it all when you get there yourself. Until then, my best advice to you is to try as hard as you can to maintain your patience, and, in the case of mysteries such as this, always strive to resist the siren call of logic.

Just like magic, my former mood of despair and hopelessness was instantly replaced by feelings of happy anticipation. *This time,* I vowed, *I definitely will not mess up!*

I paused for a moment to once again get my bearings after that bit of reflection and renewed dedication, and as I caught sight of my hand gripping the wrought-iron curlicue handle affixed to the door of the restroom, a shiver of excitement raced through my newly minted body. *Holy mackerel! By the looks of that hand, I'm a young dude this time! A young dude, and in America! It would most certainly be the most coveted assignment of all, were we allowed to covet! Oh, hallelujah and amen!*

I hurriedly pulled open the door and rushed up to the mirror with eager anticipation. Although the room was dark and littered with trash and the small mirror was clouded and streaked, I was thrilled by the somewhat blurred image I saw reflected back at me. *Good Lord — what's this? A teenager, probably no more than sixteen years old! And not a bad-looking dude at that!* I reached back and flipped the light switch near the door, but the room remained in semidarkness, the only light emanating from a small, barred window high above the sink.

In spite of the dimness of the room, I was still able to appreciate the individual features of my face. My mouth was perfect — just wide and full enough, with firm and healthy lips. My teeth were flawless and whiter than white. I loved my misty gray eyes, and my skin was clear and clean-shaven. My hair was dark brown and straight but compensated for its plainness by falling rakishly over my forehead. *No tight, scroungy curls with a bald spot on top like in Paris this time, thank goodness! Zounds! There is absolutely no comparison to that fat little middle-aged French guy I was back in '97. Man, that clown just couldn't cut it. And this time, I may have at the very least a sporting chance with the ladies!*

Whoa! What was I *thinking*? I immediately tried to toss that thought from my mind, but all my efforts were in vain. Try as I might, I simply could not suppress the vivid images of the beautiful women of Paris that came flooding back to me, and I was suddenly overwhelmed by feelings of breathless freedom and unbridled joy. What more proof was needed to tell me that I was no longer in Heaven, subject to the restraints of our exalted positions, where Angels (as you students of the faith are well aware), like men and women in Heaven, are forever single, and never yearn to marry!

After taking several minutes to calm myself, I stepped back from the mirror to get an overall view of my splendid young body. *Ye gods! I must be almost six feet tall!* I impulsively tried a few jumping jacks on the spot, almost bumping my head on the ceiling in my exuberance, and then I bent from the waist and touched my toes with ease. *Excellent physical shape, as far as I can tell.*

That's when I first noticed the purple rucksack bouncing around on my back. *Ah, what's this?* I slipped it off and set it down on the sticky floor, out of the way, under the hand dryer.

Did I say hand dryer? Was that actually a *hand dryer* there, attached to the wall alongside the sink? I must say that I feel very sorry for you Americans, still forced to put up with those useless (and sometimes downright *dangerous*) contraptions in public restrooms. You must grow so impatient with them — how at first you always smack that huge start button in a spirit of cooperation, but then, after yet another futile attempt at rapidly rubbing your wet hands together as instructed by the simple diagrams on the machine, you always end up wiping them on your shirt or your trousers, shaking your head, and — if you're like me — muttering over and over, "Stupid, stupid dryer!"

But I wasn't about to let something like a *stupid, stupid dryer* infringe upon my hitherto upbeat mood. I instinctively glanced at my watch — or, rather, at my wrist, where I would naturally expect to *find* a watch. And there it was! Thankful that I had arrived fully accessorized, I noted the time: 8:33 AM. Fully accessorized, yes. But with the cheapest little watch I ever saw! All it told me was the time! I didn't even know what day it was, let alone the year. Furthermore, it would have been nice to know exactly *where* I was — if, indeed, I was in the U.S. of A. *But that's okay*, I told myself. *As Angel Jake would say, All in due time, all in due time.*

I jabbed my hands into my front trouser pockets, eager to see what they contained, but I only came up with a handful of American change and a key ring with just two keys attached: the first was a car key with the familiar VW design, similar to the one I had in Paris, while the second one appeared to be a house or apartment key, or maybe even the key to an office or garage — it was hard to say. In my back pockets I found a pretty beat-up brown wallet, a black fine-toothed comb, and a clean white handkerchief embroidered in blue with a small *NS* on one corner. *NS,* I thought. *Hmm. Most likely my initials. Now, what could they possibly stand for? No Soap, maybe?* I had to laugh out loud at my own quirky sense of humor, even though I knew that I would just have to wait and see what name would be revealed to me. What a drag. I could only hope they wouldn't saddle me with something obscure from the Old Testament, like Nebuzaradan or Nergalsharezer.

I flipped open the wallet and was relieved to see more than several twenties — plus a couple of fives and an American two-dollar bill with slightly smeared words written on it with a red marker. It took a few minutes to decipher it, but I finally figured it out. It said:

BON VOYAGE
from your Best Buddy Jake

Well! That was very nice of ol' Angel Jake. But, on the downside, there was *no* driver's license and *no* Visa or ATM card. How was I expected to survive on that small amount of cash — plus, of course, my wits? Without a driver's license or any other identification, I had no residence address at all, which could mean only one thing. Well, two things, actually: either a bed and place to sleep would turn up before nightfall or I would be constrained to "miraculously" disappear until morning — which, nowadays, simply means finding a suitable Dumpster or hiding out under the bushes until morning.

Yo, Jake? Forget something? You remembered a car key, but where's the car? And my driver's license. What about that? Actually, on my last job I loved to drive. The Parisians are fearless drivers, and their cabbies are crazy for sure, but for me — with the knowledge that my body was just a façade and that I was, in truth, an eternal and indestructible spiritual being — driving was always a lark. But why the French drivers seemed to feel the same way about it was a mystery to me.

I was about to return the wallet to my pocket when I noticed some tiny gold-lettered engraving right on the fold: *Happy Birthday, Noah.* Well, there was an answer regarding my name, or at least half of it. *Noah!* I stuck the wallet back in my pocket and looked again at my reflection in the mirror, leaning forward until my forehead practically touched the glass. *Noah,* I whispered. *Noah. It suits me just fine.* I playfully gave myself a little wink and started to walk away, but at the last second I remembered to check between my teeth for a bit of wayward spinach or other greenery. *(Oh, that embarrassing incident in Paris with the salesgirl in the cigar shop!)*

Now, alert and confident, I was ready to emerge from the men's room like one of those rare and beautiful newly hatched bowerbirds in the dense New Guinea forests that I saw in the *National Geographic* while I was waiting for the Princess one morning in the doctor's office. (And *no*, for your information and in spite of all the ugly gossip and rumors, she was *not* pregnant in Paris! The truth is, she just went in because of this little problem she had — well, actually, if you'll excuse my saying so — it's none of your business why she went in, and I'm sorry I brought it up.)

CHAPTER FOUR

As I EXITED THE RESTROOM, the sweet scent of chocolate and cinnamon mingled with the slightly abrasive odor of overheated grease immediately told me that I was neither in a restaurant nor an ordinary bakery. No, this had to be a donut shop, no question about it. But I still had no idea what city I was in, let alone what state.

I sauntered over to the display case as if I knew exactly what I was doing and took note of the counter guy. As a stranger in a strange land, I couldn't be too careful. He looked harmless enough, though, dressed all in white, sitting on a stool and leaning back against the glass doors of the cold-drinks refrigerator case, holding a newspaper up to his face. I had only been standing there for a few seconds before he quickly lowered his paper and walked up to greet me. He was short and wiry, with nervous mannerisms and a quirky smile.

"Uh," I started, pointing to the case, "I guess I'll have that chocolate frosted one and the one with the sprinkles, and a large coffee, too, please."

He put the donuts in the little basket and set it on the counter. "We just have one size coffee," he said, placing a steaming mug next to the donuts.

"Okay." I handed him one of my twenties, picked up my stuff, and started to turn away before remembering that I had change coming. That was kind of embarrassing. But hey, forgetting to take your change happens to everyone sometime or other, doesn't it?"

There were six or seven small round tables in the place, but they were all taken except for one over in the corner by the window. So that's where I went. I placed my coffee mug on the table, along with the little red basket containing my two donuts, and used my napkin to brush the crumbs left by the previous occupants into my hand. I was half standing and half sitting, pondering what to do with the crumbs, debating whether to just let them fall to the floor like you people do, or walk over, Angel-style, and deposit them in the nearby trash container. The answer turned out to be a no-brainer: I was a human now, so why not act like one? Without a second thought, I found myself nonchalantly brushing my open-palmed hands together alongside the table, allowing the crumbs to fall where they might. No sooner had I sat down than I was startled by a tenor voice with slight nasal overtones speaking to me from out of nowhere.

"Ah! *Noah!* I found you!"

At first I thought I was hearing from *Up Above* — if you get my drift — about to be chastised for my thoughtless action with the donut crumbs, but when I looked up, I was amazed to see a guy about my age, his smiling face crowned by the most wondrous abundance of blond curls I had ever seen, tumbling wildly down over his ears like golden waves in a wind-tossed sea.

I was almost blown away by the sight. It was so magnificent! I had never seen *anything* to compare with that head of hair, even in our *Perfection Catalog of Everything: The Ultimate Spiritual Reference Book of Totality in Idealized Form* — which is available, I hasten to add, only in Heaven.

The kid was peering down at me now, his brow wrinkled and his thin-rimmed glasses riding down his nose. "You are *Noah*, aren't you?" he asked. Then he quickly added, "Hey, I *know* you are!"

"Yes, that's my name," I replied cautiously, bracing myself for the familiar sharp, swift pain somewhere in my head — confirming my immediate suspicion that this unlikely teenager was *The One* — the person I was sent to watch over, to guide, and, ultimately, to save.

But where was my sign? My proof? *Jake? Angel Jake? Wake up, please, and give me the sign! Is this my guy? Is this My Second Chance, My Latter-Day Redeemer, My Ticket back into the good graces of Heaven's elite?*

Earthly seconds ticked by, but still no sign was forthcoming from Up Above. Something was very wrong. An uncomfortable and foreboding shiver ran through my body. I have often been known to underestimate the dark powers of The Evil One. Had I once again fallen into that trap? *Could this be the work of The Devil? How else could this hirsute stranger come to know my name?*

I could feel the sweat begin to ooze from my palms and my throat start to swell with fear and panic. But just before I closed my eyes to ask for God's saving grace, I saw the kid stretching his arm out in front of my face. And there, nesting in the palm of his hand, was a small, wallet-sized card encased in a plastic holder.

"Angels Camp, California, huh?" he said, glancing first at the card and then at me. "Mark Twain territory, right?" He paused a second, grinning widely, and handed me the card. "So, how far does *your* frog jump?"

I had no idea what he was talking about. I took the card from his hand and immediately saw that it was a California driver's license — complete with a fine photo of my smiling countenance. *Oh, jeez! It must have dropped out of my wallet while I was in the restroom.*

The name of my supposed town jumped out at me. *Angels Camp*, California! Just as the kid said. I couldn't believe it! A stupid in-joke! I could *kill* those Angel Spirits up there, except for the small fact that they happen to be eternal.

But the guy was still going on about Mark Twain — a name that had a familiar ring to it, although in a kind of muffled way, like when you're trying to make out a far-away neon sign on a foggy night. You can see it, but it never becomes clear enough to read.

"I had to write a term paper about him last year," the

kid was saying, pulling out a chair and sitting down —
without, I might add, so much as a by-your-leave.

I had taken out my wallet while he was talking, but
since I didn't want to let on to him that I had never
actually *seen* my own driver's license before, I quickly
stuck it in with my folding money and put the wallet back
in my pocket.

"Who?" I asked. "A term paper about who?"

"Mark Twain. I was just saying that I had to write a
report about him — parts of which my teacher didn't
appreciate at *all*." He smiled one of those half smiles,
like it was more unpleasant than funny. "Actually, I had
to get the head of the English Department to stand up
for me, pointing out that "Captain Stormfield's Visit to
Heaven" was a legitimate part of Twain's writings, even
though his sardonic views regarding Angels and Heaven
were, uh — let's just say controversial?"

My ears perked up a bit at that, and I could feel my
hackles rising at the implied criticism of my life and
my work, but I was too busy scanning my brain for any
insight at all regarding the town of Angels Camp to pursue the matter further.

I brushed my hand lightly against the left side of my
head with the hope of sparking some sort of response,

but to no avail. I finally decided that the name of my town probably had no significance whatsoever and that I was correct in attributing it to mere game playing on the part of my superiors.

One little thing I did notice during this whole episode, however, was the guy's teeth, especially when he flashed that wide grin at me before he produced my driver's license. Unlike his hair, his teeth were quite ordinary. Actually, his bottom ones were slightly crooked and not nearly as white as mine.

CHAPTER FIVE

I DECIDED I SHOULD PLAY IT COOL with this newcomer; whoever he was, he was there for a reason. He didn't bother to tell me his name, and I didn't ask. And then he did another surprising thing. He had come up to my table from behind, and before he sat down, he'd been standing so close to me that I hadn't seen what was dangling from the end of his arm. But then he suddenly reached down and swung it up onto the table and slid it over to me.

"Forget something?" he teased, with a kind of comical maneuvering of his sprightly dark eyebrows, which, as I suddenly noticed, were absolutely incongruous with his flowing blond hair.

Oh, no! My rucksack! How could I have left that behind in the men's room! Stupid, stupid me! Rambling on about

the hand dryer and forgetting what was under it! Which was
nothing less than some of the items specifically chosen and
packed for my needs! I couldn't believe it! I'd been here less
than an hour and already I was messing up! And this guy
was treating it all like one big joke on me!

"Your driver's license was in that outer pocket there,"
he said, motioning with his thumb. "I didn't go nosing
around in your stuff, in case you were wondering."

"Oh. No, that's okay," I answered, all the while
drawing the rucksack toward me by the shoulder strap.
"There's nothing much in there, anyway," I added,
quickly checking the zippers and then setting it down at
my feet.

He shrugged and began running his fingers through
that wild excess of hair. That was *so* annoying! But just to
demonstrate to him that I didn't care — that I was with-
drawing from the competition, so to speak — I brushed
back from my own forehead the wayward dark brown
strands that, moments before, I had thought were fairly
attractive in a Devil-may-care kind of way — if you'll
excuse the expression.

I took a sip of coffee, which was still hot enough
to burn my extrasensitive tongue, but I didn't let on.
Instead, I tried to act bored, even though I was dying

(so to speak) to see what was in that purple rucksack and wishing that this kid, whoever he was, would take a powder.

I decided to just keep mum and let him speak first. I gave him ten seconds, tops.

"Expecting someone?" he asked, right on schedule.

"What?" I tried to put a bit of petulance in my voice. Maybe he'd take the hint and bug off.

"You keep looking out the window. Like maybe you're waiting for someone."

If he only knew, I thought. If only he knew that I *was*, indeed, waiting for someone — someone as yet unknown — someone in mortal danger, destined to be rescued from an equally unknown threat, by me!

"No, not really," I answered, taking a short breath. "I'm not waiting for anyone."

It was difficult for me, telling an outright lie so soon after my arrival. But just give me another day or two — I'll loosen up.

Pretty soon he stopped looking out the window and began to drum his fingers on the tabletop. "Actually, *I'm* waiting for someone," he announced, as if it mattered to me. "It's this girl I've been sort of dating for a few weeks now."

He made it sound like that was something to brag about — dating a girl for a few weeks — and that he expected me to pin a medal on him or something. Instead, I feigned a big yawn and idly glanced around the room. But my inattention didn't seem to faze him.

"We've met here at Angelo's for donuts a couple of times before, but this is really a special Saturday —"

Did I hear that right? Did he say Angelo's? "Did you say Angelo's?" I broke in.

He gave me a blank look. "Yeah, Angelo's." He raised his arms and swung them around in a wide circle, indicating the whole store. "You know. Angelo's. Where we're *at.* Right *here.* Look at your coffee mug. What does it say?"

I glanced down at my mug. "Oh. Huh! What do you know? I didn't even notice that. So — what was that you were starting to tell me? Something about this being kind of a special Saturday or something?" *I'm going to get you for this, Jake. I mean it!*

"Oh, nothing. Just that this is a special Saturday. The first day of summer vacation, and all that."

Ah! The first day of summer vacation. Useful news at last!

He smiled, obviously at the thought of the girl, and then he broke out in that kind of laughter — part chuckle

- 33 -

and part giggle — that's so typical of teenage guys on the brink of manhood. The sidewalk cafés in Paris were full of them, especially during that fateful summer of '97.

He leaned forward now, one elbow on the table, his chin resting in his hand, ready to confide in me. "She said she'd be *happy* to meet me here again this morning, *if* she couldn't think of anything better to do."

He stretched back and yawned then, and started to rub his bare arms with his hands as if to pump up his circulation. How tanned and thin they were, his arms — protruding like sturdy wooden baseball bats from his short-sleeved sky-blue T-shirt.

"What a character she is!" he was saying. "Slightly flaky, but sweet. Gets on my nerves sometimes, though. Which is kind of surprising, you know? When I first met her, I thought she'd *never* get on my nerves." He paused, considering. "But I guess that's what happens after three weeks."

I shrugged. "Yeah. I guess." But what really interested me now was his shirt. For the first time I noticed that it was embossed with a cartoon character of a pitcher winding up on the mound and the words THE LOS ANGELES ANGELS OF ANAHEIM spelled out in bold block letters.

Wow! Talk about a helpful hint! *Thanks, Angel Jake! It's about time you started to let me know where I am. At least my choices are now limited to two! I'm either in Los Angeles or Anaheim, California. Right? The baseball shirt isn't exactly clear on that point.*

Naturally, I hoped it was Anaheim, since it's common knowledge in all of Heaven that the original Disneyland is located there. You might find this difficult to believe, but sometimes we are hard-pressed to compete with "The Happiest Place on Earth!"

Wow! I thought. *Maybe I'll have a chance to actually go there on this assignment! Wouldn't that be cool?*

I came out of my short daydream as quickly as I had entered it. The kid was glancing at his watch, which was huge and glittery gold, with a million little knobs and dials — a hundred times better than mine. Naturally, he had to fondle it a little more than was necessary for merely checking the time. He suddenly stood up then, and I breathed a silent thank-you, believing that he was about to leave.

"Hey, Noah," he said. "I'm a little early, so I'm going to get some coffee and say hi to Angelo. Save my place, okay?" He playfully knocked on the tabletop with his knuckles, as if that somehow gave him the legal right to return.

Save his place? What nerve!

Sure, I admit it. I *was* put off by him — not only by his attitude, but also because I didn't know anything about him. Was he necessary to my mission, or just a passing distraction? I mean, how can I do my job when I'm left completely in the dark on matters like this? It's just not fair, when it would be so easy for those spirits in charge Up Above to supply me with all the information I needed! The only reason I can think of for them not doing so is that they want to keep me on my toes. They want me to know that I'm more than just a mere robot. They want me to remember that I'm an *Angel*, by God!

That's probably why I really resented this kid's appearance so much. I mean, who was supposed to be the Angel around there, anyway! With that hair of his, all that was missing were his wings, for gosh sake!

But hey, listen to *me*! I'd only just arrived and already I was speaking as if I were one of *you*! As a matter of fact, Angel wings are just one of the many fanciful fabrications that you people have dreamed up throughout the years.

Oh, I don't mean *you, personally.* But it's really pitiful, the things that *some* of you dream up. Don't get me wrong. Like I said, most of you have had nothing whatsoever to do with all the mistaken info regarding Angels that's been circulating around for ages. Man, those Italian artists were the worst! I can understand how they must have loved painting those wings on their Angels, and maybe they were just ill informed or ignorant about the wing thing, but all the same! Or maybe the artists figured that their Angels just looked better with some kind of visible means to keep them floating around in the clouds and preventing them from falling to earth. But either way — whether the reason was ignorance or aesthetics — it just wasn't right!

The gospel truth (in case you don't know) is that the *seraphim* are the ones with wings. They have three pairs of them, actually. And the *cherubim* have wings as well, but just one pair each. As for the rest of us lesser Angels, well, use your head, okay? It takes more than a pair of *wings* to get from the Kingdom of Heaven to other places in the universe.

Actually, if you want to know the truth about Angels, you must look in the *right* book — if you get my meaning. Go to the *source* — that's my advice. But whatever you do, always beware of charlatans. Believe it or not, some of those people who write books about Angels and their personal experiences with them are just blowing smoke. Here's a helpful hint: if they refer to the *seraphims* or *cherubims*, that's a dead giveaway. Just toss that book out as fast as you can, because there are no such words! It's all very simple. The plural form of *seraph* (the highest order of Angels) is ser*aphim*. No *s*! And the same with *cherub*. Two or more of them are called *cherubim*. Again, no *s*! Cherubim are the second-highest order, right below the seraphim. If you want an earthly analogy, it's something like a senior's relationship with a freshman. Well, not really. But it's something like that. Anyway, thanks for allowing me to vent on this. It really grates to hear those same mistakes repeated year after year after endless year.

CHaPTer SIX

AFTER THE KID LEFT, I WAS EAGER to see what was in my rucksack, but first I spent a few minutes looking out the window, trying to get a feel for the neighborhood I was in and a general impression of the people walking on the sidewalk outside of the shop.

Something I hadn't noticed before caught my eye; directly across the street was a three-story office building with a fairly large sign over the door that said NEV-CAL SAVINGS AND LOAN COMPANY — LAS VEGAS BRANCH. Now *that* was peculiar. And then I took a closer look at the cars driving by on the street. Most of them had Nevada license plates! What was going on here? Had I been misled by a T-shirt? Was it possible that I *wasn't* in LA or Anaheim at all? That I was actually in Las Vegas, Nevada?

And then came the clincher. An officer of the law had just walked through the door and was making her way to the counter. Her partner was double-parked outside in a car clearly marked LAS VEGAS METROPOLITAN POLICE. I couldn't believe I was stupid enough to get fooled by a shirt on someone's back. (I hope you'll agree that this is one incident that should remain strictly *entre nous*.)

Wow! It was hard to believe I was actually in Las Vegas, Nevada! Sin City itself! Oh, the hair-raising tales I'd heard "back home" about this place — stories relayed to us Angels by the spirit-bodies of fallen women who were led astray into vice and degradation, but saved just in the nick of time by repentance and grace. Yet how fond are their memories of their unsaved companions! And how wonderful it is that the knowledge that their former bosom pals and friends are burning in eternal Hell and damnation for their unrepented sins does not dampen their *own* enjoyment of Heavenly bliss one little bit! Such is the power of goodness and righteousness!

Buoyed by these musings, I vowed to resist with all my powers the earthly temptations that I myself might encounter during my sojourn into this sinful land, but at the same time allow myself to be open to the innocent joy and beauty that surely must exist there as well.

Once the initial shock of my actual whereabouts had subsided, I decided it was *really* time to see what was in that rucksack of mine. I lifted it onto my lap and zipped open the smallest of the three compartments, the place where the kid said he'd found my driver's license. It was empty now. *So why didn't I remember my rucksack when he produced my license in that overly dramatic way of his? What is wrong with me, anyway? I'm just a stupid, incompetent fool!*

I had to struggle with the zipper on the middle pouch since it was stuffed to the brim with books. I pulled them out and placed them on the table. There were five in all, plus the little spiral-bound daily planner that Angel Jake always sends along with me. *But wait! Why am I being so hard on myself? It's not that easy, this Angel business! And coming here as a teenager is doubly challenging! Our uncertainties, our insecurities, our hormones! I should give myself some slack! After all, I'm doing the best I can!*

I picked up the first book from the top of my little pile. Seeing its title was like a knife thrust right through my heart: *The Bodyguard's Story: Diana, the Crash, and the Sole Survivor.* Surely, that wasn't given to me to *read.* What could it possibly tell me that I didn't already know? Fighting back tears, I quickly set it aside.

The next two books were paperback travel guides called *Winky's.* The one on top was for Las Vegas, but would you believe the other one was a guide to *Paris?* And it was a used copy to boot — dog-eared pages and under-lined passages and everything. Boy! Talk about rubbing it in! Somebody up there wasn't *about* to let me forget!

And then, adding insult to injury, there was a stained and tattered textbook entitled *Second-Year French for American Students.* I couldn't believe it! My French was impeccable.

The next book looked very intriguing, however, since it was about me (well, *us*). It was called *Guardian Angels: Our Friends in Need,* and it was by someone named Dr. Stanley J. Featherstone. (Naturally, I was familiar with Reverend Billy Graham's excellent classic, *Angels: God's Secret Agents,* but I had never heard of this Stanley Featherstone character.)

Last, of course, was my trusty drawing pencil, a couple of pens, and the familiar spiral-bound daily planner, in which I was expected to record the events of my stay.

Setting the other books aside, I quickly read the introduction to *Winky's Las Vegas Guide.*

Las Vegas is located in the state of Nevada in the U.S.A. and is often referred to as Sin City. The main thoroughfare is called the Strip, which is perfectly appropriate since it encompasses in one simple syllable the bold and brassy character of this twenty-four-hour, anything-goes, girls-and-gambling neon metropolis blooming in the Nevada dessert.

Dessert? I laughed out loud at the image implied by that misspelled word. *Las Vegas, plopped down in the middle of a chocolate mousse? Fantastic!*

I wondered if Angelo's Donut Shop would be listed in the book. I quickly thumbed through the index and saw that it was — on page 33. But it was actually listed under its full name: Angelo's All-Day All-Nite Donut Emporium with Internet Access.

Well, that "Internet Access" part was news to me. I glanced around the store and sure enough, there they were — several computer terminals against the wall around the back of the place, just across from the restrooms.

What a wake-up call that was! *You're going to have to be much more observant than that, buster, if you expect to save some lives around here before you go!* I took my own advice and scanned my surroundings with eagle-eyed determination.

What do you know? There was my new acquaintance, Mr. Hair, all hunkered down in front of one of those computer screens, thoroughly engrossed in whatever he was viewing. I paused a moment to make inner contact with my own new adolescent-boy persona, and it immediately became clear to me what he was looking at: *naked women!* Or *worse.*

It took me a minute or two to sort out my reaction. I hoped it was condemnation that I was feeling, but I feared it was more like envy. A wicked and Evil thought suddenly flitted across my mind, like a spark bursting free from the fires of Hell. *Maybe I should stroll over there and see exactly what he is looking at.*

I was about to act on that ill-conceived impulse when my pal and protector, Angel Jake, stepped in just in time to nip in the bud that Evil error in judgment. In this case, his modus operandi (to use his own favorite phrase) was to direct my gaze to the large poster that was hanging to one side of the row of computers. I hadn't seen it before since my view was blocked by this attractive but extremely plump lady sitting at the table next to me. But Angel Jake must have decided that she had eaten enough donuts for the day and sent her packing. Now the poster was in plain sight. And what a poster it was! It featured a silhouette of a voluptuous nude woman, framed by a large red circle intersected by a wide diagonal slash that covered most — but not all — of her, uh, well, you know what I mean. Block letters at the bottom of the poster spelled out the warning: STRICTLY ENFORCED! Its message for the Internet users was unmistakable.

Try as I might, however, I simply couldn't stop myself from glancing up at that poster from time to time, just to make sure I understood what it meant.

Get a grip! You know what it means! It means you're a liar and a — uh, a liar and a pervert! That's what! I took another sip of coffee, but it had grown cold and slightly bitter. *Wait! That's not fair! I am a teenager, after all! What do I expect?*

Suddenly I had the feeling that everyone in the place was watching me, and snickering, waiting for me to look at that poster again. Pointing and whispering about me. But a glance around the room proved that wasn't true. I could have been invisible for all they cared. After a moment or two, I faked a yawn, heaved a huge sigh, and turned to page 33 of *Winky's Las Vegas Guide.*

ANGELO'S ALL-DAY ALL-NITE DONUT EMPORIUM WITH INTERNET ACCESS: Conveniently located just two blocks away from the famous Vegas Strip, "Angels" is a down-home, friendly place with excellent coffee, great donuts, and just enough Formica tables to make it feel cozy. The proprietor, Angelo Ramirez, may be recognized by some as the former Sergio the Singing Waiter on the hit TV show of the '80s called *Whooping It Up at Wayne's.* Upon hearing the show's famous catchword (*Ka-Boomsy!*) Sergio was required to drop everything he happened to be carrying — a loaded serving tray, a huge vase of flowers — and always, his trousers. The entire nation was shocked when he suddenly and unexpectedly stormed off a live taping of the show, saying he was sick and tired of the ridicule and vowing "to strangle" the next person who dared to use "that word" in his presence. That was the end of his show-business career.

I glanced over at the counter and took another look at Angelo. *Gee! Who would have guessed?*

I shoved all the books back in my rucksack except for the one about Angels, and opened it to a random page somewhere in the middle.

Oftentimes, I read, *when little children are taken from us, they become God's Special Angels upon their arrival at the Pearly Gates.* I might have laughed at the absurdity of that statement, except that it was *so sad.* The Pearly Gates reference was true enough — they're an eye-catcher for sure — but really, God doesn't turn children into Angels! Why *would* he? He created all the Angels he needed before he created man! Furthermore, our numbers are constant! Angel Jake's wry comment again raced through my mind: *Some of the things you people believe just don't make a lick of sense!*

I flipped the book shut and reread the name of the author on the cover: Dr. Stanley J. Featherstone. *What a clueless panderer, playing into the hopes of grieving relatives! Going to Heaven should be consolation enough! No need to be God's Special Angel! Boy, how I would love to get a chance to set that guy straight! Holy sheesh! And this is supposed to be the scientific age! Unbelievable!*

So far so good. I didn't find any big clues or hints regarding my future moves in my rucksack yet. Nothing like the city map that I found in my Paris *sac à dos*, with the Ritz Hotel circled in red and just enough money for the cab ride over there clipped to it! (Angel Jake came up a little short on the tip, however, but I added to it from the change that I found in my pocket.)

My pack was still lying across my lap, so I stood it up on one end and peered into the last pouch. *What is this then?* It seemed to be a small bundle of clothing, but when I pulled it out, I was surprised to see just a pair of shorts and a T-shirt wrapped around one of those huge thirty-two-ounce soft-drink cups with the lid firmly attached. *Whew!* I thought. *Something sure needs washing in here!* If they were going to supply me with a pair of shorts and a T-shirt, you'd think it would be clean! *Thanks for nothing, Jake! These duds smell to high Heaven!*

But the real shock came after I gingerly removed the plastic lid on the cold-drink container. *Great balls of fire! What was* this! *A huge dead* frog, *shoved in headfirst, with its long, muscular legs twisted around its green slimy body like a double-jointed ballet dancer who had danced herself to death — emitting an odor that immediately reminded me of the underground sewers of Paris!*

I hastily replaced the lid on the container and quickly rewrapped it with the shorts and T-shirt. Then I stuffed the bundle back into the pouch and zipped it shut.

Holy Moses! What was that *all about?* I mean, I'm not that squeamish about frogs. Jeez, I had eaten *plenty* of their legs in Paris, and they were very tasty, too, I might add. But a *dead* one, in my rucksack! Now *that* was a horse of a different color!

But then I suddenly remembered the rule: there is a purpose for everything and everything has a purpose. That deceased amphibian was not useless baggage! Anything but! It was just an early but quite puzzling addition to my sparse and highly inadequate arsenal of useful tools and weapons for this, my current assignment.

I lifted my rucksack off my lap and was placing it on the floor next to my chair when I noticed that something was stuck to its leather bottom. A gentle touch and there it was, right in my hand — a piece of grimy, crumpled paper, obviously torn from some sort of magazine or catalog. I didn't have a chance to examine it too closely because at that very moment I was unexpectedly hit with a double whammy that almost did me in.

First of all, I was seized with a stomach cramp, the likes of which I had *never* experienced before — keeping in mind, however, that I have no distinct memories of my many previous assignments throughout the entire six-thousand-year history of the world. (No distinct memories, that is, except for Diana, of course, as well as the many experiences I had there in Paris and the many interesting characters I met along the way. Yes, I believe that I am destined to remember Diana — and Paris — throughout eternity.) But be that as it may, even *more* painful than the stomach disturbance was the sudden recurrence of that familiar cramp on the left side of my head that I described to you earlier.

As usual, the head pain was fleeting, but the knives churning in my gut precluded any further procrastination. I quickly zipped open one of the compartments of my rucksack and stuffed the folded piece of paper into it, and the next second I was off and running to the john, leaving my rucksack behind on the floor, my empty coffee cup on the table, and the last bite of my second donut still in the little red basket.

CHAPTER SEVEN

MY EMERGENCY TRIP TO THE MEN'S ROOM took longer than I'd expected. It was partly my fault, of course. I should have known better than to break in my tender new stomach with coffee and a couple of sugary-sweet donuts. Herbal tea and maybe just a bite or two of a plain cake donut would have been a much wiser choice. But it was too late to do anything about that now.

When I finally came out of the restroom, I saw that the kid had returned to my table, which was no big surprise. But now he was joined by the girl he had told me about earlier. She was holding his hand and munching on what appeared to be a chocolate buttermilk bar, but at that distance I couldn't be sure.

As I paused there for a moment to check her out, that familiar shooting cramp in my head alerted me that I was about to be zapped. Since the actual pain and duration of these Bulletins from Above — as I jokingly refer to them — varies tremendously in proportion to their importance and urgency, I never quite know what to expect. Now, however, I was alarmed by that typical short-lived feeling of numbness that invariably precedes my most powerful and debilitating attacks, usually on the left side of — *Oh, God help me! Here it comes!*

I stumbled backward a few feet so I could partially lean against the wall until the pain subsided.

Just as I expected, the force of this attack accurately predicted the importance of its message. Even though The Girl was sitting with her back turned to me and I couldn't see her face, I knew for certain that *she was the one.* I took a deep breath, straightened my shoulders, and brushed back my hair. I was prepared for anything.

Ha! What a joke! There was no *way* I could have prepared for what I was about to see as I circled around her table and caught my first full view of her face. There she was, sitting with her head bent slightly downward in that oh-so-familiar pose, looking up at me from under that marvelously blonde and shiny crown of hair, with those huge eyes of hers meeting my own with her endearingly shy but flirty gaze. *Diana! O Diana! What are you doing here?*

For a few fleeting but wonderful moments I actually believed that my golden Princess was still alive. Her violent and bloody death in that highway underpass was nothing but a terrible, horrible dream. There were no days and weeks of mourning, no sad regrets for what might have been. And most of all, there was no one to blame.

But like all brief and shining moments, it was not meant to last. Reality returned like an annoying and unwanted guest, flooding my brain with painful memories. Even now I can see the great outpouring of notes and flowers and teddy bears blocking the entrance to Kensington Palace in remembrance of the People's Princess. I still can see the streets lined with stricken mourners weeping in each other's arms, and the non-stop television coverage of Diana, Diana, Diana — her storybook wedding day, the blissful times that followed, the birth of her sons. And then, the troubles — the

other woman, the rumors, the gossip, and the lies —
troublesome times that I refused to watch.

The heartrending testimonials that followed that
fateful night were heard not only to the ends of the earth,
but all the way to Heaven as well, causing even the Angels
to weep — but in a strangely *happy* way, since even weeping Angels in Heaven are basically happy down deep
inside of them where it really counts, and where happi-
ness *always* dwells and all the songs are sweet.

"Hey, Noah. Are you okay?" It was the kid, leaning forward in his chair and lightly touching my arm.

"Huh? What?"

"You look kind of funny. Are you okay?"

"Oh, yeah! Well, I was just feeling a little dizzy there
for a moment. Too much caffeine, you know. It always
does that to me. I'm okay now, though."

That was a lie, of course. As a matter of fact, I was still
struggling to recover from the crazy, mixed emotions that
were rattling around in my brain. Unlikely as it seems, I
suddenly found myself recalling — in ultrafast motion —
the way the chef in the open kitchen at Jon-Pierre's on
the Rue de la Paix used to shake around a mess of chicken
giblets in a bagful of seasoned flour before frying them.

He would clamp his hands around the top of the bag and shake the life out of those suckers — the little puffs of flour escaping from the bag like steam from a volcano about to erupt. My brain was just like that faux volcano, except that it had already erupted! Boy, was I angry! What a dirty, rotten trick to play on me! Of all the girls in all the donut shops in America, they had to send me one who looked and acted so much like the lovely Princess whom I had deserted in her most desperate hour of need. But then, when I bounced that bag of chicken innards around some more, I suddenly became the most grateful dude in all the world.

I'm sure that Angel Jake had a hand in assisting me back on an even keel after the absolutely shattering way he had pointed out my newest assignment — in the flesh. I'm also sure that it was chiefly because of Jake's intervention that I was able to face — in a more-or-less normal manner — the two young people sitting at that table.

"Here, have a seat," the kid said, pulling up an empty chair from an adjacent table and placing it *between* himself and The Girl. Now, *that* was an unexpected surprise, until I came to the realization that since there were three of us at that round table, *anywhere* I sat would be between them. (Such is the magic of the number three in conjunction with a geometric circle — a delightful thought that would never have occurred to me Up Above, since, of course, there is no math in Heaven.)

"Ah, Noah," the kid was saying, patting my shoulder while giving The Girl a sideways wink. "You had me worried there. I thought that maybe you'd gone off and carelessly left your backpack behind, *again.*"

What a patronizing and snide remark! I shrugged it off, though, without taking my eyes off The Girl, even for a second. Fully recovered by then and ready for duty, I let loose with my number-seven smile. I have ten practiced ones altogether, but number seven is the most complex of the bunch. Above all, it is *sincere.* It is also very focused and friendly — a smile that can be counted on. Yet, at the same time, it is not at all pushy or intimidating. It says, *I am intrigued by you, and I would gladly follow you to the ends of the earth, but I would never, ever stoop to harass or stalk you in any way.* As you might imagine, it is a very difficult one to pull off — except for at that moment, when every little nuance of my expression, from the sudden sparkle I knew was in my eyes to the sexy poutiness of my lips, came directly from my honest but temporary-on-loan heart.

The kid hesitated for just a second, but I could tell that he had somehow tuned into the vibes that were already reverberating between The Girl and me, and had deftly changed our blossoming cozy twosome into a permanent threesome. He spread his arms wide and enclosed the three of us in a tight little circle. "Noah," he said, glancing first at me and then at The Girl and then back at me, "meet my good friend, Barbra DeMarco."

Then he looked back at her in such a sweet, personal way that it sent a slight shiver of reluctant admiration through my body. *How does he do that? There goes my number seven, right to the cellar.*

"Barbra," he continued, "this is Noah, an old buddy of mine. We first met in the Tijuana jail during spring break two years ago, and then we were able to renew our friendship at the Juvenile Detention Facility last summer." He gave her a big smile and another wink.

I tentatively extended my hand to The Girl. *I must be friendly, but not too friendly.* "I'm very pleased to meet you, Barbara."

She grasped my hand and let out a kind of nervous high-pitched laugh before she spoke. "Glad to meet you too, Noah," she said. "Any friend of Andy's is a friend of mine. But my name is Bar*bra*, not *Barbara.*"

Although I can't remember ever being doused with a bucket of ice-cold water, I believe that I experienced the exact same effect at the sound of her laughter and voice. Or, to put it another way, her shrill laugh had erected the guillotine, but her actual spoken words were like the sharp blade unmercifully falling upon my fully exposed and vulnerable neck. *Where, oh, where was the laugh I had anticipated, a laugh as soft and gentle as a Paris breeze in April? And what had happened to the dulcet tones and elegant refinement of My Lady's native tongue?*

I must have been in a state of shock, because I could only sit there at that round Formica table and stare into the beautiful blue eyes of this girl who *looked* so familiar but who *sounded* like a creature from another planet. (Which, when I stopped to think about it, was about the size of it.)

Obviously, she had no way of deciphering the real reason for my distressed look, so she must have assumed I was still confused about her name. "You know — *Barbra,*" she explained. "*Funny Girl*? 'Second Hand Rose'? That Barbra."

Funny girl? Secondhand rose? What was that *supposed to mean?*

She suddenly hunched her shoulders and leaned

forward, jutting out her beautiful neck, and started singing very softly, almost in a whisper, *"Father has a business, strictly second hand . . ."* and then continuing with
something about toothpicks and a baby grand. As Angel
Jake would say, it didn't make a lick of sense.

She stopped and glanced at me with a quizzical look.
I noticed that Andy was looking at me the same way. They
were both waiting for me to respond, but I was still in the
dark. I had at least two choices: I could either pretend
to get it ("Oh, yeah! Now I see!"), which could get pretty
risky in case either one of them carried on with further
references. My other possible choice was to maintain a
very straight face and pretend to *pretend* that I *still* didn't
get it. So that's what I did. I just sat there, trying to look
like I knew what was going on, but that I was pretending
I didn't. It is a complicated maneuver, but one that often
comes in very handy in the Guardian Angel business.

Finally, I couldn't stand it any longer. I had to say
her name, even though it was under my breath — *Diana,
Diana.* I caught Barbra's eye and held it.

"Do you mind if I ask you something?" I started,
innocently enough. "Did anyone ever tell you that you
bear a remarkable resemblance to Princess —"

"Princess Diana!" she exclaimed. She suddenly

reached over and gave Andy a sharp poke in the ribs. "See! What did I tell you!"

Andy sucked in his breath and bent over in exaggerated pain. "Hey, watch it," he said. "I've got a stomach of steel, but still."

"Oh, sorry. But what did I tell you!" She looked back at me. "People are *always* saying how much I look like Diana!"

Andy just rolled his eyes and glanced up at the ceiling. "And I'm always saying, *Who cares?*"

An uncomfortable silence followed until Barbra decided to change the subject herself. "Hey, who wants to go outside and get a copy of the new issue of the *Las Vegas Daily Doings* for me?"

Naturally, I looked at Andy, expecting him to oblige her, but he merely shrugged, gave her a blank look, and leaned back in his chair.

What to do now? I thought. I wanted to help, but I was confused. Where would I look? What was it that she wanted? The Las Vegas something or other? I shrugged, too, imitating Andy's gesture, but with a bit more finesse, if I do say so myself.

"Oh, great," she said. "Thanks a lot, *gents.*" She made

a face at us and stuck out her tongue. "'Then I'll do it myself,' said the little red hen.'"

And with that she rose from the table as gracefully as a real princess and hooked her finger under the strap of her huge pink purse that was hanging from her chair. I don't know how she did it, but the way she first stuck out her tongue and then slipped that strap around her shoulder was so incredibly sexy that it actually made me gasp for air. She paused for just a moment and smiled down at me, as if she knew exactly what I was thinking. Then she raised her hand and gave us one of those quick little flickering finger waves like movie starlets do whenever they happen to spot a camera pointed in their general direction. Then she turned on her heel and headed for the door.

Andy and I watched her go in silence, while my mouth fell open at my first glimpse of her backside in all its full-length splendor.

Let me put it this way: if her blue shorts had been cut any shorter, they wouldn't have been there at all. They were topped by a wide belt made of silver coins linked together with shiny new copper ones. Her blue knit top, sprinkled with sparkling diamonds, was cut so low in the back that it barely skimmed the top of her bra. Her shoes were not really shoes at all, but high-heeled, short white cowboy boots that reached up only an inch or so above her ankle. All in all, I believe I would be safe in stating that my Princess would not even be caught *dead* wearing such an outlandish outfit as that! *Good Lord! What am I saying?*

"Hey, how *'bout* that?" breathed Andy, making a low whistling sound as he exhaled slowly through rounded lips and shaking his hand as if he had just touched the burning bush itself. "Really *something*, huh?"

Even though I felt the same way, it was all I could do to keep from smacking him. But, of course, that would never do. It was obvious to me, as it must be to you, that I needed this guy. As long as The Girl — Barbra, that is — was going to be spending time with him, I needed to be there as well. Remember, she was in mortal danger, with only me to protect and save her! My challenge was clear: befriend Andy, bond with him, and above all, never, *ever* pose a threat.

But wait! What have I done, letting her out of my sight! I immediately closed my eyes and made contact with Angel Jake. *It'll only be a minute. She's just stepping outside to get a paper or something. Help!*

My assurance came swiftly, not in a head cramp this time, but in the form of an unmistakable double beat of my heart. *Whew! Thanks, Jakey.*

Not only did Jake handle that little emergency, he also came to my aid by suggesting a clever way that I could prove to Andy that I was *not* a threat — that I would not be tempted to take his girl away from him, even if I could.

"Hey, congrats, Andy boy!" I exclaimed, immediately putting my (Jake's, that is) new plan in action. "That Barbra is really *some*thing! How long did you say you've been seeing her?"

He looked down, modestly shrugging one shoulder. "Oh, a few weeks now. Let's see — our first real date was on a Wednesday." He paused, kind of murmuring to himself and counting off on his fingers. Then he snapped them and said, "Well! What do you know? It's actually been *over* three weeks!"

"Really!" I said. "That's great! Anyway, she's a real dish, for sure. Yummy gorgeous." I paused, just long enough to maintain his attention before flinging my mightiest stone. "Too bad she's not my type, or I could have given you a real run for your money."

Andy's head jerked up. "How's that? What do you mean?"

"Well, she's just not my type," I repeated with a shrug and a disappointed frown. "I don't know what's wrong with me, but I've always gone for the more — uh, *husky* types, you might say."

Ol' Andy knit his brows, considering. "Really? You know, I have a friend like that. He just likes the chubby ones."

I laughed. "Hey, don't knock it till you've tried it," I said, forcing out the words. I reached for my wallet. "Here, let me show you a picture of my steady. We've been together all year, and we're still going strong." I quickly thumbed through my wallet. "Oh, nuts. I guess I left it home. I always keep it right by my bedside. She's a real doll, though. Her name is Brenda —" Was I on a roll or what! One look at his expression and I knew I had him convinced. *He needn't be concerned about me.*

Now he gave me a friendly cuff on the arm and stood up. "Listen, pal, I'll be back in a minute. Save our table, okay?"

I nodded. "Sure."

He took a few steps toward the john, but then he turned back and leaned down close to my ear. "Hey, did you hear about the thief who broke into the local police station and stole all the restroom equipment? A spokesman was later quoted as saying, 'We have absolutely nothing to go on.' "

I burst out laughing, and I didn't even have to pretend.

Andy gave me a quick thumbs-up and headed back toward the men's room. *You know, this may actually turn into a beautiful friendship after all.*

FROG JUMPING
CONTEST
OF
Angels Camp

CHAPTER EIGHT

THEY WERE BOTH BACK AT OUR TABLE in a few minutes, and
Barbra immediately spread a tabloid-size newspaper out
in front of her and began to read with her head bent low
and her eyes about six inches away from the table.

*Well, look at that! She's as nearsighted as a bat in a
cave,* I said to myself, suddenly recalling a phrase I had
overheard from a group of American tourists sitting at
an outdoor table at Fouquet's, a very ritzy café on the
Champs-Élysées in Paris.

In a way, though, her nearsightedness was kind of
endearing to me. Just as with her earthy laugh and voice,
it helped me to think of her more as a genuine real-live
girl than a warmed-over look-alike princess.

It was about then that Andy got the fidgets, moving his shoulders up and down and drumming his fists on the tabletop in an annoying little rhythm of his own making. Soon his leg joined in, jiggling along with the beat. And then he started clearing his throat, several times in rapid succession. I just had to laugh, because suddenly I was back in Paris (*again!*) revisiting a scene in an old French film called *Les Vacances de Monsieur Hulot*, which a friend and I saw one evening after Diana had retired for the night. (Naturally, I had arranged with Jake to put her on Protective Surveillance before I left for the theater, and I kept thinking of her throughout the evening.) Anyway, in the movie, Mr. Hulot tries to start up his ramshackle old roadster with a hand crank in the middle of this road by the seashore, and the whole car shakes and rattles and coughs (just like Andy!) before the engine finally takes hold. This guy I went to the movie with told me afterward that he thought the old car was a 1924 Amilcar, but I had never heard of that make of automobile before.

I guess I did actually laugh out loud, comparing Andy to that car, because I felt him nudging me and asking, "What's so funny?"

"Huh? Oh, nothing. I was just thinking of something." I paused. "Hey, did you ever hear of an old car called an Amilcar?"

He gave me a blank look. "An Amilcar? What's that?"

I shrugged. "Oh, nothing."

Andy shrugged, too, and then he heaved a huge, bored sigh and stretched out his arms, managing — *accidentally* — to brush the back of his hand against Barbra's upper arm.

She moved her shoulder slightly as if warding off a fly.

"So, Barb — what do you want to do today?"

She didn't even look up.

"Barb?"

"Mmm?" She continued reading.

Andy rolled his eyes at me and tried again. "I *said*, what shall we do today? It's our first day of summer vacation. We should celebrate."

Still no response.

Andy tried yet again. "Want to go swimming? A movie? What?"

She shrugged and turned another page, still engrossed in her reading.

Although he didn't speak to her this next time, he leaned really close to her and bared his teeth like a wild animal while a low, threatening growling sound came from deep within his throat. It was all for my benefit, of course, but even so it was pretty funny. I started to snicker, but then I put my fingers up to my mouth and stopped before I overdid it.

In the meantime, Andy had placed his hands on the back of his neck and was running his fingers upward through that blond mane of his. He lifted his chin and shook his head like a — well, like a prize stallion about to be taken to stud, to put it bluntly. I turned away. Why did he have to show off like that? It was kind of sickening, you know?

"So, Noah. When did you get here?"

I looked back at him. He was sitting up straight and erect now, all business, directing his question at me.

"Uh, what do you mean?"

"I mean, when did you *get* here?" He glanced at Barbra. I could tell by his tone of voice that he was running out of patience. "How long have you been in Vegas?"

Think fast, I thought. *Think fast. Here come the questions.* "Uh, not long," I answered vaguely. Then, stalling for time, I closed one of my eyes and opened the other one as widely as I could. Using my middle finger, I gingerly swiped an imaginary loose eyelash from the outer corner of my opened eye. *Come on, you guys! Angel Jake? Somebody? A little help down here, okay?* I took another couple of seconds to quickly rub my fingers together, flicking the offending lash onto the floor.

"Did you drive all the way down here from Angels Camp, or what?" Andy persisted.

"Yeah, I drove down yesterday." *That's brilliant! So where's the car, you big liar?* "This guy I went to high school with, well, he moved here last year and he invited me down. But then after I got here, I found out that what he *really* wanted was to borrow my car for the weekend!" *Not bad. Not bad. Keep it going.* "I'm not sure when he'll be back."

"Are you staying at his place then?"

"Well, I thought I was. I mean, I had *planned* to. I was hoping he'd show me around. I've never been here before," I added, finally making *one* true statement after all. "I stayed over there last night, but his mother and her boyfriend weren't exactly overjoyed at having me." I hesitated a moment, shaking my head. "It's a pretty bad situation — lots of screaming and stuff. I could see why Jeff wanted to get out of there. I sure don't want to go back."

I took a deep breath and exhaled through my mouth,

kind of puffing out my lips, trying to imitate the way people do when they've pretty much had it. I quickly speculated what his next question would be. Probably something about my immediate plans. But Barbra suddenly chimed in, her voice ringing with excitement.

"Oh, *wow!* Look! The Psychic Fair starts today! Over at the Mirage Hotel." She tapped her fingers on the full-page ad and shoved it over to Andy. "See? It starts this afternoon at two and goes on until seven this evening. And then it's open again tomorrow, from ten AM until midnight. Let's go, okay?"

Andy made a face, as if he were smelling some of those French cheeses that cost an arm and a leg at Fouquet's. "Why would we want to do that?" he asked. "Those guys are either quacks or money-grabbing fakes, or both." He smiled, obviously pleased with his choice of words.

Barbra pursed her lips, taking her time, considering her options. She slowly rotated her shoulders in a relaxed kind of stretch, then turned to me with a hopeful smile. "Hey, maybe *you* want to go —"

Andy immediately began to blink very rapidly, and he cleared his throat again. He watched her closely as she began running her fingernail along her lower lip, flaking off the dried lipstick.

"That's okay with you, isn't it, Andrew?" she asked. "If Noah comes along —"

I really had to hand it to her. Calling him *Andrew* in a kind of haughty way. Man, oh, man. She was miles ahead of him.

Andy shrugged. "I guess so," he mumbled.

Barbra touched my arm. "Well? What do you say?"

I tried not to show too much enthusiasm. "Sure. I could do that. I don't have any plans for today, or anything. Come on, Andy," I urged. "It'll be fun."

He shrugged one shoulder. "Okay."

Naturally, I was overjoyed. Now I would be able to remain close to her without resorting to hidden miracles, like becoming invisible, for instance, which is an extremely difficult trick to pull off nowadays. You may even say it's *impossible,* as far as I'm concerned. There was still Protective Surveillance, of course, but I know by sad firsthand experience how that process can be fraught with pitfalls. So being able to actually *be* with her was the best possible solution.

"Some really famous people are going to be there," Barbra went on. "Like Gloria-Marie, for instance. Have you ever heard of her?" She looked at me first, then at Andy. "She's this really great spiritualist! She gave me a reading last year. God! She knew all about me! It was amazing." She paused, staring off into space with this faraway look in her eyes. "She really helped me a lot."

"Yeah, right," remarked Andy, his voice oozing with sarcasm. He pushed the paper toward me. "Here," he said. "Enlighten yourself."

A spiritualist? What's that all about? Sounds like The Devil's doings, to me. I skimmed down the long list of names in the ad, which was divided into columns with headings like HEALERS, PSYCHICS, SPIRITUALISTS, ASTROLOGISTS, MASSAGE THERAPISTS, MEDIATORS, INTUITIVE READERS, CRYSTALS, and AUTHORS. And suddenly, from the AUTHORS column, a name practically jumped off the page and hit me in the eye: Dr. Stanley J. Featherstone! Popular author of *Guardian Angels: Our Friends in Need.*

"Hey!" I exclaimed, truly surprised. I pointed to his name in the ad. "I have a book by this guy! What a *charlatan*! I'd love to meet him and tell him exactly what I think of him."

"Great!" said Barbra, leaning over and planting a big kiss on Andy's cheek.

His eyebrows shot up and he turned toward me with a wink and surprised little shrug.

"It's still a little early, though, isn't it?" I said. "It

doesn't start until two — right, Barbra? So what'll we do until then?" Before they had a chance to answer, I gave them my own suggestion — something I had thought up even *before* I had asked them the question. "Gee, maybe you guys could show me around the town. I mean, I've never been here —"

"Okay!" she broke in, her voice bubbling with enthusiasm. "We can be your tour guides." She looked at Andy. "Right?"

He pursed his lips and cocked his head to one side. "Sure. Why not?"

Barbra picked up her purse by its long strap and slipped it over her shoulder. "I'm going to the restroom," she said. "I'll meet you guys outside in a few minutes. Okay?"

Andy stood up as she was walking away and brushed off the seat of his trousers. "Obviously, she doesn't know the meaning of the word *charlatan*. I don't understand how she can fall for that psychic crap." He paused. "But then again, maybe I do. She's a little spacey sometimes. It's just so *annoying*, listening to her spouting off about the weirdest things. She even believes in Angels, for God's sake!"

Ouch! That hurt! But I bit my tongue and didn't let

on. "Yeah, I see what you mean. But still, it can get to be pretty boring, being with someone who agrees with you all the time. At least this gives you two something to talk about."

"*Argue* about, is more like it."

"Yeah. Well, you know, I found out the hard way, with my first girlfriend, back in the seventh grade, that there *are* ways to discuss things without actually *arguing*. Maybe you should practice that a little before you two —" *What am I doing? Giving advice about something I know absolutely nothing about? Sheesh! What next?*

"With your first girlfriend, in the seventh grade, huh?" he said, cutting me off right in the middle of my sentence. "Mr. Experience, that's you."

"I guess you could say that." *Oh, dear God. If only that were true! Due to circumstances beyond my control, I don't yearn to marry in Heaven, and I'm not allowed to on earth!*

Andy gave me a quick cuff on the shoulder. "Listen, champ, I'm off to the john again. Time to give my hair a good combing. See you outside in a minute, okay?"

His hair! Can you believe it? How vain! But wait. This could be my only chance to go online and look up some of those things they had referred to that I didn't know anything about, like jumping frogs and funny girls.

I glanced over at the computers and saw that one of them was not in use, so I rushed over there and got to work. I only had a scant few minutes to accomplish my task, but I was pretty sure I could do it. First, as I soon discovered, "Second Hand Rose" was a hit song of the 1920s that was revived in the late sixties, when it was sung by Barbra Streisand in a stage play — and later in a movie — called *Funny Girl.* So that was all coming together quite nicely. Obviously, Barbra was named after Barbra Streisand. But why? Who can say?

As for Andy's question, *How far does your frog jump?*—that was easy to find: an annual frog-jumping contest is held in late May at the Calaveras County Fairgrounds, just outside of Angels Camp, California! *So if today is the first day of summer vacation for the kids, this year's event must have been fairly recent.* Reading on, I was surprised to learn that the frogs in the contest routinely jump eighteen, nineteen, or sometimes even twenty feet! That certainly is much farther than what is stated in our *Official Specification Book of Amphibians on Earth!* Or wait. Do we really have such a book? Maybe I just dreamed it. Sometimes things get a bit murky after I've been down here a while.

I needn't have worried about the frogs, though.

Further reading on the frog-jumping site revealed that the winning "jump" at the Annual Frog-Jumping Contest at Angels Camp is actually the *combined total* of three consecutive jumps! Further proof that sometimes you people just can't be trusted. (Present company excepted, of course!)

Before I signed out, I found myself somehow mysteriously connected to a site I never clicked on or even asked for — an older posting about hot-dog-eating contests in America. It was there that I learned that on the Fourth of July, 2007, at Coney Island in Brooklyn, a young American named Joey Chestnut halted the six-year-reign of the world-record holder — the talented Mr. Takeru Kobayashi of Japan — by consuming the astounding number of sixty-six Nathan's hot dogs *and* buns in just twelve minutes! Picture that!

How did you humans ever *survive* — before the invention of the Internet — without invaluable information like that at your fingertips? (Ha-ha. Just kidding.)

I signed off the Internet and gave a wave of thanks to Angelo for the free use of the computer. I had a really funny feeling then — a genuine déjà vu moment — if you know what I mean. It was like I already had at least an inkling about all that stuff I had just learned (except for the hot-dog-eating champion — that was entirely new). Maybe I could have even recalled at least part of it *without* the Internet if only I had concentrated more and given it a little more time.

But enough of that kind of speculating. I hitched up my trousers and threw my rucksack over one shoulder. I was so excited that my mouth was actually watering. And what a new and weird sensation that was! In fact, I was surprised at how much I had missed *all* bodily fluids during my absence from earth. They can be a pain in the neck sometimes, and messy as well, but still — you don't miss things like that until they're gone.

But now, here I am, a teenager in Las Vegas, Nevada, about to be shown around the town by a couple of my peers — a would-be Romeo and a very beautiful girl. What more could I possibly ask for!

chapter nine

I WAS JUST LEAVING ANGELO'S, making my way toward the door, when I happened to catch sight of Barbra and Andy through the large window at the front of the shop. They were talking with their heads close together, all the while keeping a close eye on the door.

What could they be up to? They must be talking about me; why else would they be keeping watch on the door like that? I fooled them, though. I quickly stepped outside, trailing close behind some big guy wearing a cowboy shirt, and I confronted them before they had time to see me coming.

They both looked up so suddenly you'd think they'd just heard a blast from Gabriel's trumpet.

"Yep," Andy was saying, shoving his hands in his pockets. "It's at least ninety degrees out here, even in the shade." He looked up and acted as if he were surprised to see me. "Don't you think, Noah? Ninety degrees?"

"Ninety, at least!" I agreed, pretending I didn't suspect a thing. I glanced at my watch. It was almost ten o'clock. "And so early in the morning, too. Is this, uh, typical for around here?"

"Pretty much," answered Barbra. She dug into her purse and pulled out a pair of pink-and-white sunglasses. "We *are* in the desert, you know." She slipped on her shades and adjusted her hair. "The Strip's over that way, just a couple of blocks. Let's go."

"Wait a sec," Andy said, stepping in front of us and blocking our path. He put his arm around my shoulder and herded me over to the recessed entrance of a little souvenir shop just a few steps away. Barbra followed close behind.

I began to panic. *Ah! I knew it! Here it comes. They must be on to me! But that's impossible — isn't it? Neither one of them would have any reason to suspect that I was an actual Guardian Angel, for Saint Pete's sake. And even if I did come right out and confess the truth to them, the chances are about a billion to one that they would ever believe me.*

At least Andy wouldn't. I'm not so sure about her, though. But heck, except for his glasses, Andy himself looks more like an Angel than I could ever hope to, and she sure doesn't suspect him.

I tried to keep my voice steady as I read the little sign propped up inside the shop window:

HOURS: Noon to Midnight — Every Day

I glanced at Andy. "What is it? What do you want to show me? It says there that this store doesn't open until noon —"

"Yeah, I know." He let go of me then and spread his hands out in front of my chest. I was ready for him, though. I had my next move all planned out, which was to duck out from under his reach and quickly escape down the street. (Of course, I would come back for The Girl later. You can be sure of that!)

Andy was hesitating. I didn't know what to expect, but I was ready. Then he suddenly raised both hands up to his own head. A little tugging, a little lifting, and *voilà*! He laughed and raised his flowing blond curls high up into the air, like a precious offering to the gods. His gorgeous mane was nothing but a magnificent wig!

"Holy *Jesus*!" I exclaimed, to my eternal chagrin. (But, hey — I was *really* surprised.)

"Here, try it on." He held it out to me with one hand while he brushed back his own short dark hair with the other. The wig seemed to have a life of its own even after Andy removed it from his head. How grand and imposing it was, like the Golden Fleece from long ago, back when humans still believed in myths.

Barbra was beside herself, jumping up and down and squealing like an excited child I remember watching in Paris as she was about to hop onto the famous carousel at the Luxembourg Gardens. It seemed as real as today — the little girl in her blue Sunday frock and party shoes, and the music of the carousel echoing in my ears.

"Go on — try it!" Andy was urging.

Quick as a flash, I was transported back from France to the sidewalk entrance of a souvenir shop in Las Vegas, Nevada. *Why am I always thinking about Paris? Can't I ever forget?*

"Noah? Did you hear me? Are you okay? You look —"

"No, no. I'm fine." I could feel something thumping in my chest. Of course! It was my heart! I was actually beginning to feel like a genuine human being again. Or, at least, how I *thought* a genuine human being would feel if he were in my place.

"I knew you'd like it," Barbra said. "I could tell by the way you kept eyeing it."

Andy was still holding the wig in his outstretched hand. "Here. Take it," he said. "Actually, I just wore it for a joke this morning, but now it's getting too hot for me under all that hair."

Just then, Barbra stepped up and took it out of his hand. "Stoop down a minute," she directed me. "I bet it'll look really cute on you!"

After she slipped it on me and I felt the softness of its curls brushing against the sides and back of my neck, I thought that I might be back in Paradise. Then I caught just a glimpse of my reflection in the store window. I carefully checked all the different angles until I found the very best viewing spot. Wow! All I needed now was a billowing white robe and a pair of wings and I could out-shine *any* of those old Italian masters! I flipped the long curls with the back of my hands and then patted it down softly, the same way I had seen Andy do just minutes earlier.

Barbra started laughing — a kind of delighted and natural laugh — not at all like the one she had demonstrated when we were first introduced. Actually, I kind of liked it.

"It's *you*!" she said. "You look like an Angel straight from Heaven, and that's all there is to it!"

My breath caught in my throat and my knees suddenly went weak. But Andy set things straight. He nodded and smiled that sardonic smile of his and said, "Yeah, he may *look* like an Angel, but that doesn't make him one!" He grabbed a hank of my new hair and gave it a tug. "Ain't that right, pal?"

"That's right!" Then I started to blabber like a ten-year-old. "This is *really* cool! It looks so *real*! Boy, you had me fooled!" I reached up and ran my fingers through the silky curls, just as Andy had done. "I *really* thought it was your *real* hair! Where'd you *get* it, anyway?"

Andy hesitated. "Doesn't matter." He began to walk away. "Come on. Let's go." Then he turned his head and called out to me like some kind of comedian relying on an overused and stale joke: "Hey, Noah. Don't forget your backpack."

"Got it right here, I *think*!" And then, even though I was wearing it on my back, I pretended to look for it, going around in circles as if I couldn't see it, like a dog chasing his tail.

Andy was great. I knew he thought I was funny, but he was too cool to show it. I was starting to like him more every minute.

I couldn't stop thinking about the wig — like how did Andy happen to have it, and where had it come from? Barbra and I were walking side by side now, with Andy a few yards ahead of us.

"You were in on this, weren't you?" I asked her quietly.

"Not me," she said, skipping along over the cracks in the sidewalk.

"Yeah, *right.*" I paused. "Do you know where he got it from? Why won't he tell me? Why the big mystery?"

She cupped her hands around her mouth as if she were about to reveal a big secret, which was funny, because she didn't lower her voice at all. In fact, she cleared her throat so loudly that Andy turned around to look at us. "It really belongs to his father." She paused, then added in an even louder voice, "He's got *lots* of them!"

Andy stopped walking and glared back at her.

"He uses them in his *work*!" Barbra tried to stifle a giggle by putting her hands over her mouth, but it came out anyway, like water escaping from a leaky faucet.

Gosh. Could she mean what I *thought* she meant? Is it possible that Andy's father was a female impersonator? After all, we were in Las Vegas! Or maybe he was one of those cross-dresser guys who just enjoy wearing women's clothes sometimes. Not that there's anything wrong with that. Heck, I used to have drinks regularly with a fellow like that at a certain bar-café down the street from the rear entrance to the Ritz. His name was Margaret (at least that's what he like to be called), and he was one of Princess Diana's *real* bodyguards from London. Off duty, he loved to wear pinafores, and he looked really great in them. Plus, he was always fun and interesting to talk to. Come to think of it, Margaret was the guy who told me about that 1924 Amilcar in the Monsieur Hulot movie.

Anyway, I was about to ask Barbra to tell me more about Andy's dad's line of work, but Andy himself beat me to the punch. "Do me a favor, Barbra, and just cool it, okay?" His voice was firm and steady, and I knew he wasn't joking with her now.

When she didn't respond after a moment or two, he leaned forward and looked her directly in the eye. "*Okay?*"

Barbra pursed her lips, considering. "Sure," she said. "That's fine with me."

Andy, apparently satisfied, started walking off again, but then he turned and looked over his shoulder at me. "Believe me, it's no big deal," he said.

I was tempted to ask him why he just didn't tell me about it then — if it really *was* no big deal. But I didn't want to push it, just as things were starting to go along so great.

"If you really want to know," Barbra said quietly, sidling up to me, "his dad is a private eye, and one of those — oh, what do you call them? Bounty hunter guys. That's it. Only, I was supposed to keep it under my hat. It's *supposed* to be confidential."

I couldn't believe I heard that right. I was shocked, to say the least. "Well then?" I asked. "How come you're talking about it?"

She stiffened. "I just didn't think it was all that important. Andy told me that his dad wanted to keep a low profile, as a safety precaution." She rolled her eyes. "Like as if somebody would *kidnap* Andy or something —"

"Hey, that makes sense to me!"

"Really?" She slowed down, looking down at the

sidewalk and brushing aside a little twig with the toe of her white cowboy boot. "I guess I just didn't think it was that important," she repeated.

We resumed our regular pace, and after a moment I said to her, "So what are you going to do about it?"

"I don't know," she answered. "Probably nothing. Maybe it won't come up again. But look! Just turn that corner and we're there! The one, the only — Las Vegas Strip!"

Andy, who was still walking a little ahead of us, stopped and waited for us to catch up. "I guess the tour starts here," he said flatly. "It's all yours, Barb."

chapter ten

"Ta-da! Welcome to Vegas!" Barbra exclaimed, suddenly throwing up her arms and fluttering her hands around like butterflies about to take flight. Her diamond-studded blouse and her belt made of linked coins sparkled in the sunlight. She began to swoop and strut around the sidewalk, using her whole body with high kicks and bends and twirls and swirls, so much like the professional dancers I watched perform at the famous *Folies Bergère* in Paris on that fateful night —

Oh, no! Wait! Diana, Diana, Diana! My blunder of blunders! My shame, my eternal regret, my unforgivable wickedness!

So now, my friend, you have become privy to my haunting secret: it was bound to come to light. On that horrible night in August of '97, the Guardian Angel chosen to watch over the *Princess of Princesses* found himself seated in the front row of the famous *Folies Bergère* in Paris, France. (And, as you know, to my eternal shame and regret, that Guardian Angel was me.)

Deadly distracted, I had simply *forgotten* to keep my powers of Protective Surveillance in force. Call it careless, call it negligent, call it stupid, call it criminal — it was all that, and more!

But still, in the quiet of the night, in the still of the universe, the same question always comes back to haunt me. Was it *really* my fault? *Entirely* my fault? For is it possible — is it *fair* — is it even *conceivable* to expect a lonely French bachelor to keep his mind entirely focused on the comings and goings of a middle-aged princess even as he happens to be seated next to his friend Margaret in the front-row center of the world-famous *Folies Bergère* in Paris, France? How was *he* to know that while he was enjoying the spectacle, the Princess was furtively speeding off into the night with her lover, a bodyguard, and their ill-fated driver — an employee of the Ritz Hotel named Henri Paul.

Oh, there I go again! Fie on me! Fie on me for even entertaining a question so cowardly and foul! Let me make this abundantly clear, for once and for all: the fault was entirely mine, and mine alone!

You must excuse me now. I simply *have to* have another cigarette.

chapter eleven

All right! Believe it or not, I feel much better now, with that unbearable load off my chest. So let me continue with Barbra and her big surprise performance.

Several guys who had stopped on the sidewalk to watch her dance began to clap and whistle and give her the big thumbs-up. They were wearing black leather jackets with pictures of motorcycles and the letters h.o.g. plastered all over them, and they all sported huge silver rings on *each one* of their fingers, plus thick silver belts and heavy key chains. But as their clapping and stomping grew louder and more boisterous, Barbra began to look more and more concerned. She abruptly finished up her routine with a modest little bow and then rushed over to

Andy and me. She squirmed her way between us, hooked one arm around each of us, ducked her head down, and started pulling us up the street at a very fast clip. "Come on, guys," she muttered through her teeth, tugging at our arms. "Speed it up."

It wasn't easy trying to stay three abreast while maneuvering in and out among the crowds of tourists going in both directions. I broke into a sudden sweat. *Great Scott! Was she being threatened back there in any way? Am I prepared to defend her? What could I have done?* I shuddered just thinking about what could have happened had the situation turned ugly. I was outnumbered six to one and outweighed by at least five hundred pounds! (I would have loved to calculate the exact number, but it was *not* the most opportune time.)

However, I soon came to my senses: I was succumbing to one of our greatest bugaboos, and that is thinking like a human rather than an Angel. The only fact that really mattered is that I was *there*, fully prepared, with my holy armor intact. That is all that is required of me — of us. To be sure, the ways of Angels are clouded in mystery and are often incomprehensible to logical minds. My advice to you? *Try not to think about it!* Your job is simply to *trust and believe*, and we'll take care of the rest.

✷   ✷   ✷

"My *God*!" Andy exclaimed after we had covered a half block or so. "What were you thinking, doing *that* routine — and right out there on the *side*walk?"

I cringed at his undisciplined exclamatory excess, although, God knows, he didn't mean to be offensive. That is, I don't believe his intention was to take the Lord's name in vain. Actually, I think a case could be made for just the opposite! In his own subconscious way, Andy was merely expressing his great awe for the almighty and supreme power of God by comparing it to Barbra's wild and totally awesome performance. All the same, I am not excusing his unfortunate lapse, and I still deplore using God's name in vain, whatever the cause.

But rather than chastise her as Andy was doing, I was only curious about one thing: "Hey! Where'd you learn to dance like that? That was — uh, that was totally *awesome*!"

Barbra, still looking a bit deflated after Andy's outburst, shook her head and raised one shoulder in a half shrug. "Oh, I don't know. Just picked it up from MTV, I guess."

Andy leaned forward, still keeping up the pace, and looked past her and over toward me. "MTV, my foot! It's

- 94 -

more like she has it in her genes! Her *mother's* genes. And I don't mean just the dancing part. Take a look at her —"

"Watch it, Andy!" shouted Barbra. She glanced around at several people who had stopped to stare at her. Then she adjusted her dark glasses and added in a slightly softer voice, "Just watch it, okay?"

So what was that all about? I couldn't understand why she would be so offended at having "her mother's genes," and I couldn't help noticing how her response seemed to mirror Andy's own reaction when we were talking about his father's wig a few minutes before. Andy was aware of that, too, because he began bobbing his head from side to side like an elementary-school kid and reciting in a high-pitched, singsongy way, *"Tit for tat and tat for tit. Let that be the end of it."* I winced when I saw him acting like that. It was so childish and stupid that I felt embarrassed for him, even if he wasn't embarrassed himself. Barbra just glowered at him for a minute, but she didn't say anything.

All the same, their little public disagreement was upsetting to me. And besides that, I was still worried about those guys in their leather jackets. *Were they following us? Did they mean us any harm?* I turned my head back for a quick glance behind us, but the men were nowhere in sight. However, what I did see a little farther on after a slight bend in the road was so unbelievable that I thought I surely must be dreaming. It was either that or I had been supernaturally transported by pure Angel power straight back to Paris. For there, across the street and only a few blocks away, stood the Eiffel Tower in all its beauty and majesty!

I was completely overwhelmed. Las Vegas was truly amazing! We were walking, but very slowly now, mainly because of me, gaping at the sight with my mouth wide open. As we drew closer, I could see that tower was smaller than the original but surprisingly accurate all the same.

"Can people actually go to the top of that thing?" I asked.

"Sure," Barbra answered. "I've been up there lots of times." She suddenly got this very sheepish look on her face and smiled what I thought was a very guilty smile. She glanced at Andy. "Well, maybe not a *lot* of times —"

"No need to explain," Andy said shortly. "Hey, I know by now that you're no Angel."

My ears perked up. *She's no Angel? What was that supposed to mean?*

Barbra suddenly came to a halt, right there in the middle of the sidewalk. She put one hand on her hip and gave Andy a little push on his chest with the other. "Well, how many times have *you* been up there with someone, lover boy?"

Andy stared at her for a minute before answering. Then he started to laugh. "Never!" he said. "I've *never* been up there with *someone* — as you put it — in my entire life." He paused, then added, "Except for that time when I went up with you, of course."

"*Really?*" Barbra persisted, her tone sugary sweet. "And what about when your mom gets you a free pass?"

"What are you talking about? She *never* gets me a free pass —"

"Oh?" Barbra paused and reconsidered. Then she nodded and said, "Yes, that's right. I remember now. When you took me up there, all your mom did was say a few words to the ticket taker, and what do you know — no tickets necessary!"

Somehow they had lost me in their various accusations. *Is this romance breaking up right before my eyes, or is it just typical of teenage relationships nowadays? Changing the direction of the conversation might help.*

"But at least you guys have been *up* there!" I said,

bending my neck and gazing up to the top of the tower. "Heck, I've never even been up there *once*! I had a lot of chances, but the lines were always too long."

Andy turned quickly and stared at me with flintlike eyes. "I thought you said you'd never been here before," he said steadily, accusing me as if I were on the witness stand. He looked at Barbra.

"Yeah," she agreed, returning his glance. "That's what he said."

I held up my hands, warding them off. "No, no! I don't mean *here*! I was talking about in Paris. The real *Tour Eiffel.*"

"You've been to *Paris*?" Barbra asked. "Wow! Lucky you!"

Okay. Time to change the subject completely. It was a big mistake, blurting that out. "Shall we cross over?" I asked. "I want to get a closer look."

I was happy to see Barbra slipping her arm around Andy's waist, obviously calling for a truce. "Sure, if you want to," she said, and I couldn't help wondering what that would feel like — Barbra's arm around *my* waist. *Stop that, you Devil! Get thee behind me, Satan! I command you! (Whew. That was close!)*

I was about to head for the corner and the nearest

- 98 -

crosswalk, when all of a sudden, in back of me, all heck broke loose, if you'll excuse my expression. First, the music started, and it was really loud! Then these huge streams of water suddenly began shooting up toward the sky — and I mean shooting up *really* high! *Swoosh! Swoosh!* Huge jets of water, about a hundred of them, or so it seemed, shooting up at various intervals and then falling back into the humongous pool all bubbly and foamy, and even spraying some of the people who were standing too close, and all in time to the music.

"What's happening?" I shouted.

Andy cupped his hands around his mouth and hollered back. "It's the Bellagio Hotel. The famous fountains. Watch!"

And what a show it was! I felt really sorry that Angel Jake couldn't have been there with us. He would've gotten a big kick out of that. I mean, Heaven is pretty nice, but there are some things it just doesn't have!

I was still in a daze when the Dancing Waters finally quit dancing and the spectators slowly began to drift away. Barbra offered the thought that after living there for a couple of years, you just didn't notice all that stuff anymore. "Like that volcano up the street," she said, "blowing its top every hour, or the pirate ships exchanging cannon fire and finally sinking under the water. After a while, you just don't notice that stuff anymore."

"Volcano?" I looked up the street where she was pointing. "There's a volcano?"

She laughed. "Hey. That's just the beginning! You're in Vegas, don't you know!" She pulled me out toward the edge of the sidewalk. "Look. Can you see the skyline of New York City? It's all there!" She turned around and pointed in the other direction. "And up there, past the bend in the Strip, there's Venice!"

"*Venice*? Really?"

"Well, it's sort of Venice." She laughed. "I guess it's sort of like a Disneyland Venice."

A slight breeze had come up, and she brought a hand up to her hair to keep it from blowing into her eyes. She turned her head, very calm and collected, and began to look around. "What happened to Andy? Do you see him?"

I don't need to tell you again who she reminded me of, standing there like that, with her hair blowing gently in the breeze. But thinking about Diana suddenly made me aware of what I was supposed to be *doing* here. My call to action could happen at any moment! Could the many unique and showy attractions of Las Vegas actually be part of a diabolical plan to distract me from my duties? Was Barbra actually in impending danger? And what about Andy? What did I really *know* about him? Was I being lulled into complacency by —

"Oh, there he is," Barbra said, interrupting my thoughts in midstream. She was motioning over to where Andy was standing, in front of a rack of vending machines, mostly filled with magazine-size leaflets featuring buxom girls in various states of undress. I was shocked! Truly *shocked*! I stole a few extra glances just to make sure that I was seeing what I suspected I was seeing, but I didn't say anything, and I tried not to show it.

"Sorry to *interrupt* you," Barbra said to him, quite sarcastically, I thought — as well she should, considering the circumstances. She gestured across the busy street toward the Eiffel Tower. "But Noah wants to cross over."

Andy hastily folded the paper he was looking at and stuffed it in his back pocket. "Okay. Let's go." He grabbed her hand, motioned to me, and stepped off the curb.

What? They're going to cross right here, in the middle of the block? There are four lanes of traffic out there! Are they nuts! Or is this my moment of truth?

"No, wait!" I said, reaching for Barbra's free hand

and pulling her back. My breath was coming fast and I felt a trifle faint. "There's too much traffic! Let's cross at the light on the corner!"

I know they heard me, but they chose to ignore me.

"Wait!" I shouted again. "It's too dangerous —"

But they had caught a slight opening between a Ford pickup and a blue Buick sedan, and were already tentatively venturing out like swimmers wading into the sea between the crashing waves. Barbra gripped my hand even tighter and tried to pull me up alongside her. "Come on! We only have to make it over to the center divider!"

My mind was whirling like an out-of-control inline skater on the Champs-Élysées on a Friday night, and I was gripped by fear. *This is it! I know it!*

I didn't see the guy on the bike until he was almost on top of me. That's when Barbra suddenly jerked my arm so hard that she practically pulled it out of my body, and I crashed into her with a pretty big wallop. She was okay, though. She just threw me an irritated glance and repeated even louder this time, "Come *on!*"

In a few seconds we had landed safely on the center strip under the palms, the three of us still hanging on to one another's hands. But Andy was already edging into the street, checking the traffic on our right. He immediately found what he considered to be an opening and took off again, dragging Barbra and me along after him.

Once on the other side, we scrambled onto the sidewalk and wove our way straight across the flow of pedestrian traffic. Andy, still in the lead, pushed ahead, and before I knew it, I was standing in the midst of a completely new world — inside the opulent Gambling Casino of the magnificent Paris Las Vegas Hotel. And, wonder of wonders, The Girl was still alive! I felt certain that I was somehow partly responsible for that, although I couldn't figure out exactly how I managed to keep her safe during that extremely risky crossing. But wait! I think I might have it! Perhaps at first, when I was afraid to — well, not exactly *afraid* to cross the street, but let's say too *smart* to wade into all that traffic — and Barbra yanked on my arm and I bumped into her and all that? Well, it's possible that the drivers on the *other* side of the street noticed all the commotion, the way she was literally *pulling* me halfway across the boulevard. Well, maybe, like I said, that attracted the attention of the drivers on the other *side* of the street and made them slow down enough so as *not* to run us over! Hey, don't scoff. Stranger things have happened. For instance, how about this fellow I met in Paris who ate an airplane? You'd call *that* strange, wouldn't you? It was a Cessna, model number 150, to be exact. It took him two years to finish it, but even so! He also ate eighteen bicycles, lots of TV sets, and some supermarket carts. He just likes to eat stuff like that. His real name is Michel Lotito, but the people in France call him *Monsieur Mangetout*, which means Mr. Eat-it-all. I wouldn't blame you if you didn't believe me, though. If you have your doubts, you can always go on the Internet and check it out for yourself.

I hope you're not beginning to think I'm obsessed with food — you know, first telling you about Joey Chestnut, the American champion hot-dog eater, and now this Frenchman who snacks on bikes. It just that *Up There*, where I come from, our usual diet of manna tends to get a bit boring after the first couple of millennia. An occasional hors d'oeuvre consisting of hot dogs or chopped bicycle seats and shredded carburetors might be a welcome change. (Ha-ha. Just kidding again. Manna's *great*! *Really*!)

chapter twelve

"Ah! Air-conditioning!" Barbra exclaimed as we stepped inside the glittering casino at the Paris Las Vegas Hotel.

"Yeah!" I agreed, pinching the bottom of my shirt and stretching it out to let the cold air circulate up to my chest. "Feels great."

I looked around and saw that we were surrounded on all sides by just about every type of gambling device I could imagine — video machines, old-fashioned one-armed bandits, craps and blackjack tables, roulette wheels galore, and a seating section for bingo players off to one side. But even more than the cold air, I loved being surrounded by that unique casino sound. It's just impossible to describe, but you'll see what I mean if you ever get the chance to hear it for yourself.

I didn't understand why I was so attracted to the place. All I knew was that if anyone felt right at home in a place like that, it was certainly *moi*!

But wait! There is *one* possible explanation. Could it be a holdover memory from one of my previous assignments? Yes! I think I'm starting to remember. The word *kid* is flashing through my brain. I can almost see it now, passing through my mind, frame by frame, almost like a movie. *The Cincinnati Kid! That's it!* Believe it or not, I was once sent to watch over the famous Cincinnati Kid! Of course, he lost that memorable last poker hand, but it was for his own good.

Ah, but that was long ago. Right now, the first thing I did after the three of us had a chance to catch our breath was to reach for my wallet.

Andy grabbed my arm. "Hey, whoa there! You're underage, remember? Put that money away or we'll all end up in the hoosegow before you can say Hackensack, New Jersey."

I'm sorry, but I found that remark to be very offensive. *Who does he think he is, telling me to put my money away!*

"Underage?" I asked, like a complete ninny. "And how old is *that*?"

The funny thing is, I really didn't know! After all, I'd never been in Las Vegas before. How could *I* know the age restrictions on gambling in one little part of the world? I mean, let me ask *you*: How old must you be to gamble in — uh, let's say Krasnoyarsk? See? It's not that easy, is it? So maybe I wasn't a *complete* ninny after all. Maybe just half a ninny — a 50 percent ninny. Or maybe even just five-sixteenths of a ninny. That would be — uh, let's see — five divided by sixteen — that would be about 31 percent ninny. (Gosh almighty, but I do love arithmetic! You don't realize how lucky you are, doing math whenever you darn well feel like it.)

Anyway, Andy was giving me a *really* strange look now. "You're pulling my leg, right? Okay, I'll play along. Twenty-one is the minimum age for gambling in the state of Nevada. And *you* won't even be seventeen until next year. I saw your driver's license, remember?" He shook his head. "Jeez. I can't believe I'm telling you this. Where have you been? Hiding out in a cave somewhere? Hiding out in some long-lost gold mine, for God's sake?"

Well, what do you know! I am actually sixteen, just as I had guessed when I first saw my reflection in the mirror at Angelo's. Little by little, the facts dribble in. I glanced at Barbra and decided to try to save face once again by pretending that I knew all about underage gambling laws in the state of Nevada and that I was just having some fun with them.

"Hey," I said, pointing at Andy. "He's not kidding, is he? He actually believes I live in a cave. Like Batman."

"Batman doesn't live in a cave, you moron," Andy said. (Quite rudely, too, if you ask me.) Now, here's the thing: I don't believe people should joke around about morons. After all, they are God's creatures just like you and me, and are born for a *reason!* Some say it's to bring people closer to Him, but I really can't comment on that.

Anyway, I was about to set Andy straight about morons in no uncertain terms, but before I could even start, I was interrupted by Barbra, who had suddenly grabbed my forearm with her two hands and was raising it in front of my face. "Look," she said. "You're bleeding!"

"I *am*?"

Andy examined his own hand, the one he had grabbed my arm with. He held it out to me. "She's right. Look." He wiped off the blood with a couple of swipes on the side of his trousers.

Blood! Real blood! My blood! Can it be true? Do I actually bleed, just like a real human? Words cannot describe the way I felt at that moment. It was stupid, I know, but suddenly I wanted to hug the entire human race, even though you *are* all crazy as loons. But still, I wanted to hug all of you. *My brothers! My sisters! And now, my countrymen!*

Barbra had slipped her purse off her shoulder by then and was rooting around in it. "Wait," she said. "I think I have some tissues in here."

Andy gently took my arm again, being careful to avoid touching the bleeding area, and examined it the way a doctor might. "Ah, it's not so bad," he said, as if to reassure me. "How'd you do it, anyway?"

Is this the same guy who called me a moron a minute ago? And who now seems genuinely concerned about a little cut? What is it with these kids, anyway?

Barbra was still digging around in her purse. "I think I know what happened," she said. "I think you scraped your arm on my belt when you ran into me on the street. See, the coins are strung together with these little sharp clips —"

So! The Girl I was sent to protect demonstrates her appreciation by causing me to bleed all over myself! I had to smile at the irony of it all.

"Oh, nuts," she said. "I'm out of tissues."

I reached into my pocket and pulled out my hand-kerchief, and Barbra quickly tied it around my wound.

"You probably should go wash that off," suggested Andy. "The restrooms are way in the back, around that corner."

I nodded. "Good idea."

Barbra pointed to a long queue of people not far from where we were standing. "That's the line for tickets to the top of the Eiffel," she said. "We'll get in line and wait for you over there."

"Okay."

She lowered her head then and looked up at me from under those beautiful golden brows with that shy and flirty little smile, so like the one that the whole world had grown to love. "And, Noah," she said, touching my hand, "I'm sorry about the cut."

But this time her smile was meant only for me.

I don't know what got into me. I mean, I really *did* intend to go find the men's room and rinse off my arm, but somehow I got detained at a particularly beckon-ing row of video poker machines. I don't like to brag, as you know, but I do happen to possess a rare affinity for the game of poker — but only when I'm on duty here on earth, naturally. As you may have suspected, there is no gambling allowed in Heaven. But not for the reason you might think. It's not that gambling is sinful or immoral (bingo, anyone?). No. It's not that at all. The problem is that Heaven is a *happy* place. (Remember, all misery and anguish and pain is left behind in this vale of tears once you've arrived at the Pearly Gates.) Those of you who know a little bit about gambling and the human psyche will understand completely when I say that the irresistible urge facing the compulsive gambler is not *winning* per se, but the thrill and rush engendered by the possibility of losing. And since it is impossible to *lose* in Heaven, well, what is gambling without the thrill? Simply losing money, that's all. Albert Einstein put it best: "God does *not* play dice!" he said. What could be clearer than that?

Aside from the natural attractiveness of the video poker machines — the wide, comfortable seats in front of them, the huge screens, and the clear, colorful images of the playing cards — this one particular row of games had an added feature: it was sheltered and protected from the curious eyes of those ceaseless wanderers and souvenir ashtray pilferers wending their way among the serious players. The eight or nine machines were positioned facing the wall opposite the bar, and there happened to be one vacant place at the end of the row. But what was really peculiar about it was that the occupant sitting at attention adjacent to the empty spot was a large but friendly looking German shepherd Seeing Eye dog!

The thing is, I *love* dogs! I really do! But, sadly enough, the only time I get to see and interact with them is when I'm here on assignment. That's another pleasant thing about the French, by the way; they take their dogs *everywhere*. And they treat them as they would their children. Heck, I've known some parents over there who would leave their kids home with a nanny and take their *poodle* out to dinner! That is so nice to see. But please brace yourself now for some truly heartbreaking news, especially if you love dogs the way the French and I do. I'm just so *sorry* to have to tell you this, but the unvarnished truth is that there are no dogs in Heaven, in spite of the widely circulated but unfortunate and hugely sentimental rumors to the contrary. Nor, for that matter, are there cats or sheep or orangutans or bunnies or tigers or billy goats Gruff. Or flies or finches or grasshoppers or snakes or tapeworms. There is simply no need for lower animals in Heaven. Only those beings who possess that hard-to-define entity called a *soul* are allowed and welcomed into the Kingdom. *And why is this?* you may rightly ask. I can answer that question in only one way, and it is this: Don't ask me. I'm not the one in charge.

I approached the dog with caution and respect, and he responded in a similar manner. His master, sitting next to him, was a grizzly old guy wearing blue overalls and glasses as thick as ice cubes. I extracted a twenty from my wallet and sidled in next to the dog. "Hi, boy," I said softly, gently sliding the back of my hand against his right flank. "How's it goin'?"

The dog, immediately recognizing my true Angelic nature, lowered his head and turned toward me. "Just fine," he growled. "How're things with you?"

Okay. Hold it. Hold it just a second now. You didn't believe that, did you? Or *did* you? See, the trouble with a lot of you folks is that you tend to believe all *kinds* of foolishness. Actually, though, I don't hold it against you. How could I? How can you be expected to distinguish between what we Guardian Angels are *capable* of doing and what we are not? For instance, if one of my brethren has the power to turn back a ferocious tigress about to attack and devour a defenseless Chinese woman and her two small children (as reported by God's faithful servant

Mr. Billy Graham), it stands to reason that we *must* be able to perform such a relatively simply task as exchanging a friendly greeting with a Seeing Eye dog! Or so you would think.

But no, the dog did not respond to my overtures. Instead, the old man turned his head slightly and squinted at me for several seconds. Then he looked up toward the ceiling and slowly stroked his straggly gray beard as if he were deep in thought — before he suddenly turned toward me again and began to speak in some kind of odd dialect that is really hard to duplicate without spelling it out phonetically for you. (Oh, a bit of a warning here: perhaps if you're under twelve, you should probably skip the next couple of sentences.)

So here goes. This is what he said: "Chee-sus-cry-stand-gaudall-my-tee!" At least, that's how it sounded. Then he added the killer. "Go git a harcut, son! From the looks o' ya, I thought you wuz a gol-derned hussy."

Talk about hurt feelings! Man, I was devastated! The funny thing is that I had forgotten all about my hair. Or my wig. Whatever. It just seemed like it was a real part of me, even from the very beginning. I hoped I could persuade Andy into letting me keep it.

I could feel tears of disappointment mingled with

embarrassment gathering in my eyes. And then the most surprising thing happened. The dog leaned toward me and kissed me on the cheek! Well, he actually *licked* my cheek, but for a dog, that's the same thing as kissing, right?

"Lookit dat!" The old guy slapped his knee. "He fancies ya!"

I had to smile, in spite of my misery. Then I sniffed a couple of sniffs and swiped my nose with the back of my index finger. "He's beautiful! What's his name?"

"That thar's Lucky. I raised him up from a pup. He's the derndest mutt! Here — watch this."

Old Ben, for that was the guy's name, turned to face his poker game again and pressed the DEAL button on the screen to begin a new round. Images of five cards immediately popped up. I don't remember exactly what denominations they were, but there were at least two face cards up there.

"Okey-dokey, Lucky boy. Do yer thing." Ben winked at me and motioned toward the dog with a quick movement of his head. Then he placed his finger lightly on the HOLD button under the first card and looked at his dog. Old Lucky extended his tongue and licked his chops all around. Ben nodded and pressed that HOLD button and moved on to the next. Lucky again licked his lips. But when Ben pressed on the following three HOLD buttons in turn, the dog just sat there and blinked. Ben looked at Lucky and said, "Are ya sure?"

The dog licked his chops once again, and Ben just nodded and said okay and pressed the DEAL button.

Well, I'll be derned! I mean darned. I couldn't believe it! The two cards Lucky had told him to hold were a jack and a ten, and after the machine had dealt three new cards, Ben ended up with three jacks and two tens — a full house!

"Wow! That's really something!" I exclaimed. "But —" I hesitated, not knowing exactly how to phrase my question.

"Yeah?" Ben asked. "But *what*?"

"Well, I was just curious about Lucky. He's a Seeing Eye dog, right?"

Ben squinted at me. "So? Waddaya gittin' at?"

"He's *your* Seeing Eye dog, right? But then I guess you're not exactly blind —"

"Well, Hell no, son! If I wuz blind, how could I play poker? Use your head."

That was pretty confusing. I took his advice and started using my head, but to no avail. He was not blind, because he was playing poker. But still, he had a Seeing Eye dog. Any way I looked at it, it still didn't make sense.

"Okey-dokey, look here," he said finally, leaning over and speaking directly into my ear. "The only dogs 'llowed in here are the Seeing Eye type." He paused, winking at me again. "You git it now?"

I smiled, feeling strangely honored to be in on his little secret. "Oh! Sure!" I whispered. "I git it!"

I slipped my twenty into the money slot, and my own video poker machine suddenly came to life like a resurrected saint. I pressed the DEAL button, and five cards immediately appeared on my screen. I was frozen with indecision. It had been a long time since I'd gambled.

I looked over at Ben. "Uh, can I borrow Lucky for a minute? I'm having a little trouble here deciding what to do."

"Sure! Give 'im a go!"

Old Lucky did his chop-licking thing, and I ended up with four of a kind!

"Good dog!" I said, leaning over and giving Lucky a nice pat and a doggy hug — which was a big mistake, because there was something about my hair that really turned him on. He started out with a few tentative sniffs, but in a few seconds he was so excited he started to climb onto my lap, extending his huge paws over my legs and awkwardly half falling off of his own chair, all the while panting like a cyclist on the final stage of the *Tour de France.*

"You got cats?" Ben asked, surprisingly calm, considering the circumstances. "That's what he does when he sniffs out cat." Ben suddenly turned and looked behind him. "Oh, shee-it!" he breathed.

I turned to see what he was looking at. Behind us stood a petite brunette dressed in a dark blue business suit. "Ben," she said sternly, "just what do you think you're doing?"

Ben quickly pulled on Lucky's halter and forced him onto the floor. "Sit, Lucky!" he ordered. Lucky, being an excellent representative of his breed, immediately obeyed.

"This is your final warning, Ben," the lady said. "Keep Lucky *off* the chairs, or you will have to find another place to do your gaming!"

Ben bowed his head and answered with a sheepish, "Yes, ma'am."

Then she looked at me. And looked at me some more. "Well, well," she said. "What do we have here? May I see some identification, please?"

She phrased her request as a question, but I could recognize an order when I heard one. I immediately sensed that I was in a bit of trouble, but I felt certain I could talk myself out of it.

I hit my forehead lightly with the palm of my hand. "Oh, no!" I said. "I left my wallet in the hotel."

"I'm sorry to hear that," she said. "Perhaps you will accompany me to my office then, and we'll see if we can't straighten this out."

That's when Ben chimed in. "Actu'lly, Ms. Beverly," he drawled, "the boy wasn't actu'lly gamblin' fer hisself. He was actin' for Lucky here. He wuz like a stand-in fer Lucky." The old man laughed. "Lucky's a clever one, he is, but he jest can't manage to work the machine with his paws. Not yet, he can't."

"Oh, is that right?" said Ms. Beverly. "In that case, will you please tell me how old *Lucky* was on *his* last birthday?"

"He was four, ma'am. But remember, that's in dog years! In people years, well, I reckon that'd be around twenty-eight or thirty, at the least."

Just then, Ms. Beverly's beeper went off. "Excuse me," she said politely. She removed her phone from her belt and spoke a few words. Then she hung up and looked directly into my eyes. "You come along with me now," she said. "I don't have any more time for these shenanigans."

I didn't appreciate her tone one bit! It was out of the question for me to do what she asked. I was on *assignment*, for Heaven's sake! In fact, I should have been getting back *right then* to The Girl! Oh, what was I thinking, neglecting her as long as I did?

"I'm sorry. I can't do that," I said, noticing for the first time the badge she was wearing on her lapel — the badge that proclaimed SECURITY in unmistakable letters. "And besides, I've got twenty dollars already invested in this machine, and I just got four of a kind!"

"You'd better do what she says, son," Ben advised, leaning back in his chair and stroking his beard.

Suddenly, Ms. Beverly was all business. She carefully pointed out the set of handcuffs attached to her belt under her jacket. "I won't have to use these now, will I?"

For one stupid moment I actually considered making a break for it. I quickly looked around, surveying a possible escape route, when I suddenly caught sight of Barbra, standing just a few yards away with a distressed look on her face. I thought she might come to my aid, but instead she started looking all panicky and quickly turned

on her heel and bolted right out of sight. *Talk about grati-*
tude! Considering how I'm willing to risk everything for her,
you'd think she'd at least attempt to put in a good word for
me when I needed it the most!

Ms. Beverly had her hand on my arm (not the ban-
daged one — the other one), and although it didn't appear
that she was guiding me, she actually was squeezing me
pretty hard on the side of my wrist with her thumb and
little finger — probably a little technique she learned at
police school. She led me through a maze of slot machines
and crap tables to a nondescript door that was kind of
hidden behind a potted plant, and in a few seconds we
were in a small room with two desks, a couple of chairs,
and a hat rack. A male officer was sitting at one of the
desks, busily working at his computer and eating a donut.
(Really, I'm not kidding.)

Suddenly there was a sharp knock on the door — kind
of a code. Four knocks, a short pause, and three more
knocks.

"Come in," barked Ms. Beverly.

Who should it be but Barbra and Andy!

"Hiya, Mom," Andy said, ushering Barbra in and
then shutting the door behind them.

Mom! Did I hear that right? That lady is Andy's mom?

Now Andy was nodding to the other officer. "Hi, Chief," he said.

The other officer looked up briefly, raised one hand in a quick gesture, winked at Barbra, and grunted hello. (Even *I* knew that he wasn't the chief, but he seemed to enjoy the joke.)

Barbra said a surprisingly formal hello to Ms. Beverly, and Ms. Beverly answered in kind: "Hello, Barbra. Nice to see you again."

Then Barbra rushed over to me. "I saw you being led in here on my way back from the restroom, so I went and got Andy."

"I take it that this young man is a friend of yours?" Ms. Beverly asked Andy.

Andy stood up very straight, as if at attention. "Uh — yes, ma'am."

Barbra looked down at the floor and put her hand over her mouth, trying to hide a smile.

Andy turned toward her with a very stern look on his face. "Please!" he hissed. "This is no laughing matter!"

"All right, kids," Ms. Beverly said. "That's enough of that."

Barbra blushed, but Andy just cleared his throat

as if he had been properly chastised and was ready to behave.

Now Ms. Beverly's eyes fell on my hair and lingered there a moment. She looked at Andy. "And could *that* belong to your father, by any chance?" she asked.

Andy nodded. "Well, he said it wasn't useful to him anymore, so I thought I'd have a little fun with it this morning."

His mother nodded. "I see." Then she looked at me. "What's your name, and how old are you, really?"

Before I could answer, Andy spoke up on my behalf. "He's okay, Mom. We met him this morning at Angelo's."

Andy glanced at Barbra, looking for affirmation. "That's right," she said. "He just wanted to come here to go up on the tower."

Ms. Beverly looked at me again. "You're how old?" she repeated.

"Uh — sixteen?"

"You're not sure?" she asked, raising her brows.

"No! Sixteen! I'm sixteen." *(Whew. That was stupid!)*

"And where are you from?"

I hesitated before answering. What if she questioned me further, about my address and stuff like that? Stuff that I really didn't know. But there was no way to avoid her question. I decided I'd do my best to get out of this predicament, even if I had to apologize. "I'm from Angels Camp. You know, in California? And I'm really sorry that I tried to gamble —"

"The word is *gaming*," she said. "We don't *gamble* in Las Vegas."

"Oh, sorry. Well, *gaming*, then. I'm really sorry. I won't do it again."

"You're darned right you won't. Now you march right out of here and don't even *think* of returning to Paris Las Vegas until you're at least thirty-five years old and have a valid driver's license plus three other forms of photo identification."

"Right!" I agreed, even though I thought her require-ments were a bit excessive. "I won't. And thanks a lot."

Andy already had his hand on the doorknob. "Thanks, Mom. I'll see you later."

"All right," she said, then added, "Oh, wait, Andy. Call Uncle Buck when you get a chance. He wants to take you up in his new toy."

"He did it? He finally bought the Cessna 182?" Andy grinned and clenched his fist. "Cool! I'll call him later."

Barbra held the door open for me and patted my

shoulder as I passed through. "Whew," she whispered. "That was *close*! Another couple of minutes and you might have found yourself spending the night in Hackensack, New Jersey."

I guess she thought there was something funny about the confused expression on my face, because she just laughed and said, "Never mind. Come on. Let's get out of here."

chapter thirteen

We were back out on the sidewalk now, and I was starting to get a little worried. That was a pretty close call, being imprisoned (more or less) in the security office of a big Las Vegas casino.

"I'm sorry you didn't get to go up there," Barbra said, looking at the Eiffel Tower and lightly touching my good arm. "But it *was* your own fault, you know."

"Yeah, I know," I answered, suddenly thinking of a clever way of expressing my appreciation both to her and to Andy for getting me out of a very tight spot. "I guess I don't need to go *up* in high places," I said. "I'm just thankful that I have *friends* there."

Andy gave me a quick smile, so at least he caught my drift. *Maybe I've misjudged the guy. Maybe he's not so bad after all.*

"We can come back here tonight, if you're still around," he said. "The view is better after dark, anyway."

"You know," Barbra suggested, "we *could* go over to the Stratosphere now." She pointed to the right. "It's up that way a few blocks, on the north end of the Strip."

"Sure," I said. "If you want to. What's the Stratosphere?"

"What's the Stratosphere?" Andy mocked, raising his upper lip in disbelief. "You mean you've never heard of the *Stratosphere?*"

Be careful here! This could get tricky! Angel Jake? Angel Jake, where are you? I paused a minute before answering him, as if I were trying a little harder to recall if I had ever heard about it. Then I shook my head. "Nope. Not that I can remember — not right offhand."

Andy dropped his arms down to his side and really stared at me now. "I don't believe this! You've never heard of the one thousand, one hundred and forty-nine-foot Stratosphere Tower, the tallest freestanding observation tower in the U.S.A.! How about the Empire State

Building or the Sears Tower in Chicago? Ever heard of them?"

"Well, actually, those are *buildings*, not towers," said Barbra.

"Anybody ask you?" Andy retorted.

"Now, that was *rude!*" I broke in, without really thinking.

Barbra looked at Andy, then at me, and back at Andy again. "Yeah!" she agreed, as if it had just occurred to her. "He's right! That *was* rude!"

Andy brought his fingers up to his mouth and kind of ran his nails across his teeth. At first I thought he was going to come back at me. After all, I was supposed to be his contemporary. What right did I have to interfere?

But maybe he felt outnumbered or something, because he surprised me by kind of halfway apologizing to her. "Sorry," he said, giving her a playful punch on the chin.

She grabbed his hand and laughed, which just about broke my heart.

I decided that the best thing for me to do was resume the conversation. "I guess I'm just not into tall buildings," I said with a shrug. "Actually, I'm more attuned to caves, myself." *Not bad, not bad! Kind of light and joking.*

But Andy just couldn't get over it. "I just can't get over

it!" he said, still holding on to Barbra's hand. "People come here from all over the world to see the Strat and experience the rides up there —"

"And throw up —" Barbra broke in.

Andy acknowledged her comment with a nod, but he still wasn't about to let me off the hook. "People come here from all over the world to see it," he repeated, "and now you stand there and tell me that you've never even *heard* of it."

"Oh, leave him alone, Andy," Barbra said, coming to my defense once again. And she didn't stop there. She suddenly reached over and gave him a stiff poke in the stomach. "What if I asked you where the *lowest* point in the *entire Western Hemisphere* was — or is? Could you answer *that*?"

"Aahhk!" Andy bent over, pretending that he was mortally wounded and in extreme pain. Barbra laughed again, and even I had to smile. He *was* kind of funny. Every time she poked him or punched him, he made a little joke about it.

"Listen, girl," he said. "Everybody knows that the lowest point in the Western Hemisphere is in Death Valley."

"Yeah," she agreed. "But Death Valley is a big place. Exactly *where* in Death Valley is its lowest point, and exactly how *far* below sea level is it? Tell me that, since you're so smart."

"It's uh — well, it's this little place that I can't think of the name of right now, but it's more than two hundred feet below sea level. I know that."

"For your information," retorted Barbra, "the lowest spot in the Western Hemisphere is located in Death Valley in a place called Badwater, and it's 282 feet below sea level."

Then, closing her eyes and inhaling slowly, she placed her hands on her hips and arched her back in a long, luxurious stretch that I found amazingly sexy. But I wasn't the only one. I shot a furtive glance over at Andy, and I thought the poor guy was about to swoon.

"I was there a few years ago, so I should know," Barbra added with a huge yawn, as if she were just reporting an incidental fact.

Suddenly, I was startled to hear the first few notes of "Love Me Tender," my all-time favorite Elvis Presley song, coming from Barbra's purse! "Elvis!" I exclaimed. "My all-time favorite Elvis tune!"

It was Barbra's phone, of course. She fished it out of her purse and checked her caller ID. "Hi, Dad," she said.

"What's doin'?" She listened for a few moments and then raised her eyebrows and rolled her eyes, signaling to us that this call was entirely *unwelcome.*

"When?" she asked in an irritated tone. Then a pause. "But it's almost eleven thirty now! And besides, I'm with some friends." Another pause. "Where's Teri? Why can't she do it?" She listened for a moment and then let out an exasperated sigh, puffing her cheeks and extending her lips in a cute little pout, which, apparently, got her nowhere — she was on the *phone,* after all. "O*kay!*" she said finally. "We're at the Paris. I'll be there as soon as I can. Probably around a half hour."

She carelessly tossed the phone back in her purse and zipped it shut with such a quick and powerful tug that the little charm attached to the zipper tab came off in her hand. "Oh, *damn!*" she said. "My little leprechaun fell off!"

I glanced over at Andy. *Wake up, Andy! Ask her if you can take a look at that thing and then tell her that you can fix it! Man! What's wrong with you?*

"So, what's up?" Andy asked. "What did he say?"

Sheesh! Can you believe it? I immediately sidled up next to her, carefully took the little charm from her hand,

- 131 -

and examined it briefly. "Hmm," I said. "I think I can fix that. Why don't you stick it in your purse for now and I'll look at it later, if you want."

She just stood there for a moment, looking at me in some enchanted way as if I were a prince offering her the key to his kingdom. "Well, gosh, Noah. Thank you." She brushed her hair back from her temple. "Thanks a lot."

See what I mean? Man, oh, man! What a great teenage guy I'd make if I only had the chance! But poor ol' Andy. He didn't have a clue. I was hoping that he'd notice the effect that simple phrase *I think I can fix that!* had on her, but my hastily conceived object lesson flew right past him. He just repeated his question to her. "So, what's up?"

Another big sigh from Barbra. "That was my dad. He needs me to —" She paused for a second. "Well, he needs me to help him out this afternoon. Just for a little while, from twelve to twelve thirty, actually." She paused again. "Maybe I could meet you guys somewhere after. Maybe for lunch or something?"

"Your dad?" Andy seemed to be a little surprised. "That was your dad? Where is he? What does he want you to do?"

I was glad that Andy was asking the questions. All I

knew was that there was no way I was going to let her go off alone. *Alone, and in Sin City! No way!*

I glanced over at Andy, and then back at her. She wasn't answering his questions, so I stepped in. "Can't we come along? We could just come along with you, couldn't we?"

She looked away, blinking rapidly, then stared down at her feet. "I — I don't know," she said.

"Hey," Andy broke in, "don't be so mysterious. Where is he? What does he want?"

She stood there thinking for a minute. "Oh, what the Hell," she said, which kind of shocked me, if you want to know the truth — even though it was a fairly mild oath, as oaths go. You should've heard some of those guys in Paris. *Mon Dieu!* "It doesn't matter, I guess." She glanced at her watch again. "You guys can come along if you want to. I'll get my dad to buy us lunch afterward, and I don't mean just a burger and fries."

CHAPTER FOURTEEN

WE STARTED OFF DOWN THE STRIP with Andy and me following a few paces behind Barbra, who was weaving in and out between the other pedestrians on the sidewalk.

Ol' Andy was in a pretty playful mood.

"Yo, *No!*" he said, nudging me with his elbow.

Was he talking to me? I wasn't paying attention. I was too busy gaping at the huge big Egyptian pyramid that was looming up ahead.

"Yo! No!" he said again. "*Noah!*"

Hey! That's no pyramid! It's a hotel and casino, for gosh sakes. I looked over at Andy. "Yeah? What?"

With a quick toss of his head, he indicated three rather hefty teenage girls who were coming at us from the opposite direction. They were hooked arm in arm and dressed in matching low-cut red T-shirts and billowy skirts, and they were all laughing hysterically as they struggled to keep in step with one another.

"What do you think of *those* tomatoes?" he asked.

I gave him a questioning glance, but when he looked back at me and raised his eyebrows, I suddenly remembered what I had told him earlier about my preference in women. "Oh, wow! Now you're talkin' my language!"

A few paces more and it was my turn. There were only two girls this time, similarly dressed as the first group, but considerably less heavy.

"Hey, *Ann!*" I hissed, figuring I'd give him some of his own medicine. (And I think it worked, too, judging by the way he looked over at me with a funny mixture of amusement and annoyance.)

"Yeah?" he answered. "What?"

"Get a load of those — uh"— *think of something — anything!* —"of those zucchinis!"

"Zucchinis!" He laughed. And then he spotted the girls I was referring to. "Ah! Now that *there* is more my type!" And you know, in spite of his comical leer, he definitely wasn't joking!

Three weeks? He's been seeing Barbra for only three weeks

and already he's talking like that? No sense of fidelity? No pureness of heart? Not a good sign!

I didn't have too much time to dwell on that troublesome aspect of his personality, though, because all of a sudden Barbra led us around a corner and down a busy little side street. "This is it," she announced. "We're here."

I looked up at the marquee above my head. It was a spectacle of blinking lights, each colorful letter vying for attention during its own short burst of energy.

ELVIS IS BACK! LIVE THE EXPERIENCE!
THREE SHOWS DAILY!
AT 2:00, 8:00, AND 11:00 PM

Was I in a new kind of Heaven, or what? Elvis Is Back! I didn't even know that there *was* such a place. Man, oh, man, I really hit the jackpot on this assignment!

Barbra started to walk inside, and Andy and I followed. A uniformed ticket taker was standing next to a larger-than-life-size cardboard cutout of Elvis and chatting with a small group of ladies wearing crazy red hats. When he spotted Barbra, he waved and called out a friendly "Hi, Barb! Nice to see you." Then he gestured toward me and Andy. "Are those two bums with you?"

"Yep," she answered.

He nodded and gave her a snappy little salute and waved us right in, without making us pay or anything. Like a couple of overgrown ducklings, Andy and I continued to follow Barbra in single file through some open doorways and back to a small auditorium where several groups of people were already seated. Some of them looked to be about eighty years old. Even so, most of them actually displayed little signs of movement from time to time.

No. Wait. I'm sorry. I take that back. It was mean of me. The truth is, I *enjoy* seeing old people! Really! Although I'm the first to admit that sometimes it's pretty depressing to look at them, with their wrinkly skin and sagging muscles, not to mention their unsightly varicose veins and hairy moles. Ugh. But hey, listen! Don't worry! When you get to Heaven, you *will* shed all of that earthly ugliness, *guaranteed*! Getting old and sick and repulsive is just another vastly underestimated gift from God! I mean, when you begin to look *that* horrid and feel *that* miserable, doesn't it make it much easier for you to give up your love of *this* life and yearn for better things to come on the other side! (Hey, if you're still young, I'll bet that you've never thought of it that way before. Right?) It's interesting that one of Diana's *real* bodyguards in Paris told me about a situation in his own life that demonstrated that same general principle in a different context. (Actually, I'm talking about my old friend Margaret again, that British guy I told you about earlier. Boy, I sure miss that bloke.) Anyway, Margaret was trying to make the point that sometimes the things that make us really miserable at the time they're happening — such as the myriad irritations of growing old — are really blessings in disguise. He used his daughter as an example. He said that she was about to go off to school in Switzerland, but that lately she was starting to be a real pain in the neck. (Only he didn't say *neck.*) He told me that he had finally figured out that the way she was acting was actually *her* way of making her leaving home that much easier to bear for all of them. What a very astute observation for him to make — I thought at the time — in light of the fact that he could never remember to drive on the *right* side of the road. I wish I had a franc for every time I had to shout at him, *"Vers la droite! Vers la droite!"*

Sorry about going off on another tangent just then, but I thought that was something you should know — about old people and what's awaiting them in Heaven and stuff. Anyway, you didn't miss much of my narrative. All that happened was that Barbra had just led me and Andy to a couple of choice seats in the front row. "This is supposed to be a special half-hour show for these people from the retirement home," she explained. "It should begin in five or ten minutes. Will you guys be okay?"

"Where are *you* going to be?" I asked, once again beginning to fear the unknown. There are plenty of things that could go wrong in these kinds of theatrical settings, you know. People getting electrocuted and falling off stages, for example, or maybe accidentally hanging themselves on those pulleys and things up on the rafters. You *have* heard of *The Phantom of the Opera*, I presume? And that huge chandelier crashing down on all the people? That was *not* funny!

"Oh," Barbra said airily in answer to my question, "I'll be backstage. I just have a couple of duties back there." She turned and craned her neck, looking toward the door where we had come in. "I see they've brought in a stack of programs. I'll get you guys a couple."

"Hey, Andy," I said as we both turned and watched her hurrying back up the aisle. *(Man, oh, man. Those shorts are short!)* "Do you know anything about this?"

He shook his head. "Nothing, dude. I'm just as much in the dark as you."

Barbra was walking back toward us now, and as she passed, she tossed a couple of programs in our laps without stopping. "See you in a little while," she said, and headed straight for the stage door down at the far end of the aisle.

"Why, that secretive little rat!" Andy exclaimed as he was examining the cover of his program. "Look at this!"

I looked first at his program and then at my own, but I missed whatever it was he was referring to. "What?" I asked. "What is it?"

He pointed to the large red letters slashing diagonally across the cover: **Danny DeMarco IS Elvis Presley!** "That's her dad!" Andy said. "Barbra's father is an Elvis Presley impersonator! That little rat!" he repeated. "She never said anything about that to me! And we've been seeing each other for three weeks!"

Voilà! Here is a perfectly natural opening for me to find out more about their romance, or relationship, or whatever it is! "So where did you guys meet, anyway? At school?" I ventured.

For a minute I thought he might not answer me, the way his body kind of tensed up and his shoulders hunched over. But then he loosened up with a shrug and a quiet little laugh, like he was about to reveal something a bit too personal.

"Actually," he said, taking a deep breath and lightly stroking his chin and neck, "we met at dancing school."

"*Dancing* school?"

"Tap-dancing school. Beginners' class."

Tap-dancing school! Did I hear that right?

"Tap-dancing school? Did I hear that right?" I asked. I was about to add, "That's *weird*," but I caught myself in time, and instead I just remarked, "That's kind of, uh — unusual, isn't it? How many *guys* were in the class, anyway?"

"*Are* in the class," he corrected. "We've still got several weeks to go. But I'm the only guy. Just me and eleven girls." He grinned. "Know a better way to meet beautiful women?"

I shrugged, at a total loss for an answer. How would I know anything about that!

"I got the idea from an old Liza Minnelli movie," he added. "*Stepping Out*. It was a pretty good picture."

I was puzzled. From what little I saw of Barbra's dancing out in the street, she was certainly not a beginner. "But what's Barbra doing in a beginners' class, the way *she* dances?"

Andy grinned. "You got that right! She's one of the instructors!" He paused a moment, turning up his palms and idly examining his fingernails. "My father doesn't think much of it, though — my dancing lessons, I mean."

"Oh?"

"Yeah. Says it's a waste of time." He shrugged, as if he didn't care what his father thought. "He's a no-nonsense guy, that's for sure. Hard to impress, you know?"

I nodded, trying not to think of my own Boss, and His high standards.

"One of these days I may surprise him, though. Show him that I'm not a complete —" He hesitated, fumbling for the right word.

"Goof-off?" I suggested. "Not a complete goof-off?"

"Yeah! That'll do." He laughed — a very short, sharp laugh.

The little theater was practically full by now, with only a few empty seats left in the back. All of a sudden the lights dimmed and the music started up. It was a recorded instrumental selection, and very, very loud. Naturally, I recognized the tune. It was "Heartbreak Hotel," another one of my Elvis favorites. I just couldn't repress my urge to sing along with the music, except for one thing: I couldn't remember the words. That happens to me fairly often, and it drives me crazy. But I didn't let a little thing like a failing memory stop me. I have a great tenor voice, actually, so I gave it all I had without the words. "La-da-de-do-DUM-de-dada," I crooned loudly, until Andy whacked me one on the side of my leg.

"Oh," I muttered. "Sorry."

And then, wonder of wonders, who should stroll onto the stage but Elvis himself, his guitar hanging low on his body and his hair done up in that shiny dark pompadour, singing in that amazing voice of his that always drove his fans into a frenzy. In just a heartbeat I was in total agreement with the sentiment printed on the program cover: Danny DeMarco *was* Elvis Presley! He had Elvis's every move down to perfection, and his voice was just uncanny. At first I thought he surely must be lip-synching, but it soon became apparent that wasn't the case. The man was just amazing. Between songs he kidded and chatted with the audience, telling little stories about "The Colonel" and Graceland.

This is difficult for me to admit, but I have to be honest with you and confess that for a few minutes there I had completely forgotten about The Girl and my special assignment to watch over her and shield her from harm here on your wonderful WackiWorld. Oh, but isn't this a perfect example of the extraordinary power that music can wield on the vulnerable human psyche! How many souls has The Devil tempted with hip-hop, jazz, and rock-and-roll? (We Angels cannot be tempted, however. Otherwise, how could I enjoy Elvis so much?) But still, on the brighter side, music does have its redeeming qualities. Can you imagine Easter without "Here Comes Peter Cottontail"? Would Christmas be Christmas without "Jingle Bell Rock"?

Obviously a born showman, Elvis saved his most spectacular number for last. He teased us at first by humming a little riff, and then he slowly worked up to a full-blown blast, his whole body vibrating like my Paris landlady's perpetually out-of-balance washing machine, dancing across her basement floor. There he was, belting out the lyrics as if there was no tomorrow —"You ain't nothin' but a hoouund dog"— while at the same time — wonder of wonders — high above his head, an overgrown basset hound was balancing precariously up on the roof of a huge wooden doghouse that was being lowered haphazardly down to the stage while swinging wildly from side to side! When it was about three feet from the floor, the dog made a flying leap and landed squarely on all fours, panting and sniffing around for all it was worth. Then the dog — which, as you may have guessed, was actually a person in a basset hound costume — began to dance along to the beat, kind of hanging on Elvis's pants and jumping on him and chasing him around the stage. It was a riot, and the old people in the audience were all standing up, leaning on their canes and walkers and laughing and having a grand old time. And Andy! Man! He was practically in hysterics, he was laughing so hard. Finally, after a quick second chorus, Elvis made a desperate lunge for the dog, but missed, and the dog scampered up on top of the doghouse again. And that's when it hit me — stupid, stupid slow-witted me! That was not just *any*body dancing around in a basset hound suit! That was Barbra!

Without even thinking, acting purely by reflex, I immediately leaped from my seat like an attacking tiger and jumped up onto the stage, just as the doghouse began its death-defying ascent into the upper regions in the space above the stage. I managed to grab her around what I thought was her waist — although I miscalculated just a little, but I won't go into that — and I more or less dragged her down from the roof of the doghouse, which was now swinging around like that famous nineteenth-century Frenchman Jules Léotard on his flying trapeze, which he actually invented, and who, on 12 November 1859, performed his notorious act for the very first time at the old *Cirque Napoléon* in Paris, which is now called the *Cirque d'Hiver Bouglione*, and which I personally visited when I was in Paris on my previous assignment! Actually, there's a lot more to the story of Jules Léotard that you may find interesting. His father was a gymnastics teacher, you see, and when Jules was a baby, his parents would hang him upside down to stop him from crying, since he got such a big kick out of it, even at that early age. Léotard also designed the close, body-hugging outfit that he performed in, which several years later came to be known as a tutu. (Hey! Just kidding! It came to be known as a leotard, of course! But you already knew that.)

Darn! There I went again. Spinning off into another tangent — and just in the middle of a particularly suspenseful episode. Sorry about that. Anyway, back to my own performance on the stage of "Elvis Is Back!" When I snatched Barbra off that swinging doghouse (*probably* saving her life, but I'll never know for sure), the audience must have thought I was part of the act, because they began to applaud and cackle and poke at one another in that funny old-person, endearing way they have. I guess I was slightly stage-struck for a moment there, because I was in the process of taking a little bow (really, I can't believe I did that) when the basset hound suddenly threw its "arms" around me and tackled me down to the floor, holding me there just as the huge doghouse swung right over my head, missing me by a mere fraction of an inch. Someone pulled the curtain, and the act was over. (To thundering applause, I might add.)

Barbra, a real trouper, waited until the curtain was pulled shut before she exploded.

"What the Hell was *that* all about?" she hollered, standing up and ripping off the top of her doggy suit and shaking it in my face. "You almost got us killed!"

I was still lying on the floor, kind of in a stupor, when I saw ol' Elvis looming over me in a very threatening way. He glanced at Barbra, and speaking in an actor's deeply resonant and full-bodied voice, he boomed, "Do you *know* this freak? What the *fruc*tose is going on?"

Fructose? That's a new one on me! What does he mean by that? Is it obscene? I'm shocked! But this isn't the time or place to register a complaint.

"No, it's okay, Daddy," she said, holding him back with an outstretched hand. "I know him. It's okay." She struggled out of the bottom of her costume and threw it across her arm.

I managed to stand up then — not too gracefully, I'm afraid — and like an idiot the first thing I did was reach up to make sure my wig was still on straight. "I'm — I'm so sorry," I finally muttered, with my head bowed. "I just thought — I mean, it was just a purely reflexive, uh — a reflexive reaction I had there. I — that is, I sometimes react like that when I sense that people may be in danger. You know, in some sort of danger?"

Both Barbra and her father were looking at me with

extremely dubious expressions on their faces. I might as well have been speaking in tongues, for all they knew. (As I think about it now, maybe I *should* have!) Andy had joined us up on the stage by then, and I was still stuttering and trying to come up with at least a semi-logical reason for my actions. "See," I started to explain, "when I was a kid, maybe about six or seven, my little sister had somehow snuck outside during this big storm — actually it was a thunderstorm, with lightning and thunder cracking all around — and she had climbed up on our doghouse — well, actually it belonged to the neighbor, but their dog died, and, anyway, it somehow ended up in our yard, so I followed her outside since no one was home except us because my mother had to — well, she had to uh, run over to the library because she had an overdue book and didn't want to incur an extra fine, and, anyway, I followed my sister outside — her name is Victoria — and I grabbed her off the doghouse just as the lightning struck, and it actually caught on fire and everything — the doghouse, I mean — and ever since then, I just get real nervous when I see people climbing on top of doghouses — I mean, I can't explain it — it's just, you know — a reflex — it's like a *reflex* —" I had to stop there, as I was completely out of breath, and ideas, too.

All three of them — Barbra, Elvis, and Andy — were just staring at me with their mouths open. Finally, Barbra broke the silence: "What are you *talking* about? You can't be *serious!*"

Once again, ol' Andy saved the day. I don't know why. I suppose he just felt like it, or maybe he was hungry and wanted to go to lunch. Anyway, he threw his arm around my shoulder and said, "Hey, no harm done, right?" He looked at Barbra. "You're okay, aren't you? No scrapes or scratches? No broken bones? Then let's go eat. I'm starving."

"And just who are *you*?" Elvis asked, wiping the perspiration off his brow with the back of his hand.

"Oh, Daddy, I'm sorry," Barbra said. "This is Andy Bowman. He's one of my students. You know, in the dancing class?"

Elvis offered his hand. "Hi, Andy. Nice to meet you."

"It's nice to meet you, too," Andy said. "*Great* performance! I loved it."

"Well, thank you. I've been doing it for a long time." Elvis started to turn toward me, but then he looked back at Andy. "I think I might know your father," he said. "Buck Bowman? The pilot?"

Andy shook his head. "No. That's my uncle."

"Ah, your uncle! Small world. He's my golfing partner! He hasn't been able to talk me into going up with him in his plane yet, and judging by his golf game, well —" He let out a short, explosive laugh. "But wait! I *have* met your father. Buck introduced us one day. He's a private eye, right? Finds missing persons, and all that —"

"Yeah. That's him," Andy broke in, quickly turning away and looking up into the rafters.

Elvis started to address me. "Now, *you*," he said. "You are —?"

"Oh! I'm Noah. I, uh — I mean —"

"Are you from dancing school, too?"

I shook my head. "No —"

He cut me off, thank goodness. "Listen, no more rough stuff, y'hear? Or you're right out the door."

"Oh, *right*!" I said, raising my fist in swift agreement. "I was only thinking that she might get hurt up there, you know —"

"Yeah. You already said that." He put his hand on Barbra's shoulder. "Hand me that doggy suit, honey, and I'll take it around back. Then give me a minute or two to change, and I'll meet you and your friends out in the lobby."

"Okay," she said, tucking her blue blouse with the sparkling diamonds back into her shorts. I couldn't help watching, and when she was finished, she glanced up at me for just a moment, and I'm pretty sure I detected at least the *hint* of a little smile.

CHAPTER FIFTEEN

"HEY, BARB. I'M SORRY ABOUT THIS," said her dad as he held the door open for us at a little snack shop called Juices, just a couple of doors down from "Elvis Is Back!"

"I know I spoiled your afternoon with your friends here, and I'd love to take you all out for a nice upscale lunch to make up for it. But I've only got an hour before I have to get back to work. Some people from the media are coming over and I have to make nice to them."

Barbra gave Andy and me a helpless little shrug and touched her father's arm. "Oh, that's okay, Daddy. Some other time, maybe."

The place was fairly crowded, but there was one empty booth in the corner. Mr. DeMarco waved hi to the person at the cash register and then said to us, "Follow me." He grabbed Barb by the hand and guided her into the seat facing the wall and then slid in beside her, indicating that Andy and I should sit opposite them in the corner.

"I've been bad," I said, attempting a little humor. "So I have to sit in the corner."

Andy and Barbra just rolled their eyes, and I could understand that. It was an old joke even back in '97.

"Yeah, you *have* been bad," agreed Elvis, "and you *do* deserve to sit in the corner. But the main thing is that it's just easier for me, not being in full view of my adoring public. I hate being pestered for autographs when I'm trying to eat." I understood what he meant, because even with no costume or makeup, he still looked a heck of a lot like Elvis.

Our table already had menus and little sample glasses of the "Juice of the Day" set out. Elvis immediately picked up the one in front of him and chugged it down in one gulp, reminiscent of the way I used to dispatch my nightly jigger of *dinde sauvage* at that small bar-café down the street from the rear entrance of the Ritz that I told you about. (Now I did the same thing there at Juices, as a little memorial tribute to those far-off times. *Here's to you, Margaret, wherever you are.*)

Elvis was looking right at Barbra now as they sat side by side in the narrow booth. He shook his head back and forth as if he couldn't believe what he was looking at. "Now, you boys tell me," he began, speaking to Andy and me, but still keeping his eyes on her. "Was she great, or was she great!" He playfully grabbed her by the back of her neck and pretended to strangle her. "I would say she was *stupendous!*"

Barbra was actually blushing then, and she reached up and took his hand and brought it down to the table-top. "Oh, stop it, Daddy," she said with a little laugh, still holding on to his hand. "Basset hounds are *easy*. Everybody knows that."

Even though Mr. DeMarco looked like a slightly aging rock star, he acted more like a very proud father now. He picked up his menu and motioned for us to do the same. "They have a great hamburger, fries, and shake combo here," he suggested. "But you kids order whatever you want."

Then he leaned over and spoke softly into Barbra's ear, but loud enough so I could hear. "Thanks for coming to my rescue, sweetheart," he was saying. "With no hound dog, I was really in a bind. I hated to give up that number, especially since it was a benefit for those old-timers." Then he gave her arm a little pat. "And I *am* sorry about the lunch, but I'm really rushed today. Let's plan on Fellini's or someplace like that after the eight o'clock show one night next week. How about that?"

Barbra reached over and gave him a peck on the cheek. "It's okay, Daddy. Honest. Besides, the hamburgers here are really good."

I was so proud of her! Seeing them together, father and daughter interacting so lovingly, just made me feel good all over. But to tell the truth, the whole episode was beginning to seem so un*real* to me. For there I was, in a beautiful Angel wig, with a deceased frog in my rucksack, having lunch with Elvis Presley and Princess Diana in Las Vegas, Nevada. Except for the dead frog, if that wasn't Heaven on earth, I sure don't know what is.

Later, during a lull in the conversation, I suddenly found myself asking Barbra's father how she happened to be named after Barbra Streisand. "There must be a story there," I said, popping a French fry into my mouth.

Mr. DeMarco shot a quick look at his daughter, who just sighed and shrugged and took another ladylike sip of her chocolate shake, which, I assumed, was her way of giving him permission to say whatever he wished.

"Yes, there is a story there, but it's a fairly short one. Naming her after Barbra Streisand was mostly her mother's idea," he said, lifting up his empty water glass and flagging down our waiter, who hustled right over and refilled all our glasses. "Actually, it was *entirely* her mother's idea. You see, we met — Margo and I — on the set of *Funny Girl* in our senior year in college. You probably know that Barbra Streisand starred in the original musical, and that it was loosely based on the life of Fanny Brice?" (He didn't wait for an answer, so I just sat tight and kept my mouth shut.) "Well," he went on, "I was surprised to snag the part of her husband, Nicky Arnstein, since I was only known around school for my great take on Elvis. But no one was surprised when Margo was picked for Fanny, since she'd been such a sensation as Marian the Librarian in *The Music Man* the previous year. And the fact that she looked so much like Streisand didn't hurt. Let's see, that was back in —" He glanced at Barbra. "Uh, how old are you now, kid?"

Barbra just looked at him with an annoyed frown and slowly shook her head, as if she couldn't believe he was asking her that. Of course, he was only teasing her, because he quickly picked up where he had left off.

"Oh, yes. Now I remember. It was about fifteen years ago." He paused a moment, again glancing at his daughter, and I noticed that his eyes were misting up a bit.

"Naturally, we fell in love — her mother and I — both onstage and off. As I said, Margo was *much* more talented than me. In fact, we used to joke that our director gave me the part just because I was the only one to try out." He paused. "That's not true, of course. One other kid tried out, but his leg was in a cast."

Barbra leaned hard against his shoulder and laughed. "Oh, Daddy! Stop it!"

He gave her a quick one-armed hug. "Anyway, by the end of the run, Margo was pregnant, and I was about to become a father for the first —"

He was rudely interrupted by a sudden loud burp, followed by an immediate apology from Andy. "Sorry," he muttered, belatedly covering his mouth, and then promptly burping again. "It must be the milk shake."

Mr. DeMarco sat perfectly still for a few moments — we all did — waiting to see if he could safely continue his narrative without any further disruptions. But he didn't have to wait long before it came, the *coup de grâce* — the finishing blow — a giant rumbling belch that put the previous two to shame.

It was easy to see that Andy was totally mortified. He buried his head in his arms for a few moments and wouldn't even come up for air. I really felt sorry for him, the poor guy, embarrassing himself like that — especially in front of Barbra, but there was nothing I could do. Then Barbra suddenly burst out laughing.

Andy raised his head slightly, as if he were looking to see if the coast was clear. "Hey, what was *that*?" he asked, pretending that he was just an innocent bystander.

Barbra reached both hands across the table and patted his arms. "I *told* you they had great shakes here," she said. It all happened so fast, but all I could think was, *Oh, my! I love these people!*

"Well, that's about it," Mr. DeMarco continued. "Margo admired Barbra Streisand's performance so much in the movie version that she wrote her a fan letter, and Barbra responded! It was just a short note, but it meant the world to Margo. Anyway, we moved here to Las Vegas before Barbra was born, with the intention of getting work at one of the big hotels. I lucked out right away with this Elvis gig, but Margo, being very pregnant by then, had to wait until after our baby arrived before she could pursue her own career."

I was watching Barbra all this time, and I noticed that she was beginning to look a little distressed, blinking her eyes a lot and sighing and looking around the room.

Mr. DeMarco placed his hand over hers and continued in a more somber tone. "You know, boys, it's funny, but some people just seem to be born with greasepaint in their veins — or their arteries, or in their blood, whatever. My point is that they *have* to perform. They're *driven* to perform. The theater becomes their life. The theater *is* their life." He paused and reached over to stroke Barbra's hair. "Margo just happens to be one of those people."

"*Tell* me about it!" Barbra burst out, the sudden anger in her voice piercing straight through to my brain, instantly reminding me of an incident in the Bible — the part where Jael pounded a sharp tent peg into the temple of the slumbering General Sisera, piercing his skull and pinning him to the ground, thereby not only killing a powerful enemy but also greatly raising her status in the eyes of Jehovah God. (The tale of that feisty and crafty Jael with her mean hammer has always been one of my very favorites of all the gruesome stories in the Old

Testament, as well as a real inspiration to me in times of stress. But it was no help to me now.)

The pained look on Barbra's face was doubly heartbreaking for me, since it was so similar to the expression on Diana's face whenever she was confronted by crowds of pushing and shoving paparazzi shouting out her name.

"*Tell* me about a mother who sneaks off for auditions all over the country," Barbra was saying. "Tell me about *my* mother, who happily leaves home for months — even *years* — at a time, performing for the applause of perfect strangers!"

She was starting to sob now, and her father quietly drew her face down against his shoulder and patted her back, while signaling to Andy and me with a slight movement of his head that it was time to leave. We started to stand up, both of us confused and upset by this sudden turn of events, when Barbra looked up and murmured between sobs, "Don't — please, don't leave yet. I'll be okay."

Mr. DeMarco gave us a nod, and we sat back down. Barbra took the handkerchief that her father offered to her and wiped her eyes and blew her nose. "It's just so *hard* sometimes," she started to say, still dabbing at her nose. "It's just *hard* realizing that I never had a *real* mother."

I couldn't take my eyes off of Mr. DeMarco. There was Elvis Presley, sitting across the table from me, looking about as miserable as any human being I've ever seen, except for Barbra, of course. I felt so sorry for them that I actually found myself praying for the Apocalypse to happen, right then and there! But as soon as I had a chance to reconsider what I was praying for, I quickly reversed myself. Hey, I really didn't know for sure if *anyone* at that table had accepted Jesus as their personal savior! What if the End Time did come, and they were all left behind? And it was out of the question to simply *ask* them. I mean, it would be rather awkward at a time like that to suddenly inquire, *"Say, you guys — I've been meaning to ask. Have y'all been saved?"*

Thankfully, though, Barbra was beginning to pull herself together. "I should have given up after our Death Valley trip," she said, speaking now more to her father than to Andy and me. "Remember, that's when she told us about getting the Carol Channing part in the revival of *Hello, Dolly!* on Broadway. I'll never forget the look on her face. She was *so happy*!"

For a minute there I thought that she might lose it again, but she managed to stave it off. She returned the handkerchief to her father and glanced at her watch.

"Oh, God," she moaned. "Look at the time."

"Yeah," her father said. "I should be getting back." He stood up and reached across the table to shake hands with Andy and me. "No. No, please, don't get up," he told us, and then leaned down to kiss the top of Barbra's head. "See you later, honey," he said, and then he picked up the check and headed for the cash register.

Barbra waved him off and then looked at Andy and me. "Come on, you guys. We've got to get moving. I want to be at the Psychic Fair before it gets too crowded." She put her napkin on the table and brushed off her shorts. "I've got some very important questions to ask Gloria-Marie, and I don't feel like waiting in line all day."

Andy, who had been sitting there quietly through-out Barbra's emotional outburst, suddenly came to life. He had made a fist with one hand and was pounding it rhythmically against his mouth as if he were trying his best to maintain his silence, but finally he was unable to contain himself any longer. "Barbra, *please*! Can't you spot a phony when you see one?" He closed his eyes and jerked his head downward in a quick movement of frustration and disbelief. "Jeez! Come on! For God's sake, get real!"

"Hey, hold it!" I said, immediately coming to her defense. "Don't you think that's going a little too —"

"No, it's okay," Barbra broke in, signaling to me with an upheld hand. She smiled indulgently, like a doting mother with a misbehaving child. "That's just my Andy," she sang out. "He's not quite ready to understand the *deeper* mysteries of the universe." Then she did it: the deathblow, the finishing stroke, the *coup de mort*. With her head tilted slightly downward, she looked up at him from under that swath of golden hair adorning her brow and treated him to the old tried-and-true Diana double-eyed whammy, to which no man is immune. "But he'll come around someday," she purred. "Isn't that right, my sweet?" Now she turned to me. "All he needs to do is locate his long-lost brain." The mischievous glint in her eye suddenly turned Evil as she added loudly, "Perhaps his *father*, the famous sleuth, can locate it in his ultra-secret missing persons' file."

Oh, no! Once again she crossed the line. I closed my eyes and held my breath. *Jake! Angel Jake! Hear me, please! I need your help, and I need it bad! Do something! Don't let*

*this beautiful young romance die before it even has a chance
to blossom! Reach down to this boy and soften his cold, cold
heart!*

I opened my eyes in time to see Andy begin to smile.
With a gentle sigh of resignation, he slowly reached
across the table and took Barbra's hand in his. He pulled
her toward him until his mouth was just inches away
from her ear. "I'm sorry," he said softly, even though his
expression didn't quite echo his words.

I'm not sure if Jake had anything to do with that
or not, but to me, at least it was a step in the right
direction.

CHAPTER SIXTEEN

ON OUR LONG WALK FROM "ELVIS IS BACK!" to the Mirage Hotel, where the Psychic Fair was being held, I had an experience that really knocked me for a loop. And I'm not kidding!

What happened was that I was suddenly confronted with Princess Diana *herself*, looking just as beautiful and alive as I remembered her. She was dressed in a stunning two-piece gray suit and matching gray hat, and she was standing alone just inside the open door of some kind of store or shop — I didn't notice which — just gazing at us passersby on the sidewalk with her hands clasped informally behind her back and a serene expression on her face. I stopped short, astonished and awestruck, while

Barbra and Andy continued on without me, not realizing that I was no longer trailing along behind them.

I was completely mesmerized, standing there on the sidewalk, staring at what I thought must surely be a miracle. *Will she recognize me? What will I say to her?*

"Noah! Come *on*! We're going to be late! What are you *looking* at?" It was Barbra, coming back to fetch me. I managed to point a shaking finger at the woman in gray. "There," I breathed. "Look there. It's — it's Princess Di —"

Barbra grabbed my hand and gave it a good jerk. "So?" she asked, very sarcastically. "What do you expect? It's Madame Tussauds, for God's sake! Are you *nuts*, or what?"

It took me a few seconds to come back down to earth. I was very disappointed, but actually relieved, in a way. There were no miracles at work here, merely my overcharged imagination and an overdose of gullibility.

"Ohhh!" I said with a big, goofy grin. "So *that* explains it! But — but she looks so real!"

"Noah, *please*! When are you going to quit acting so dumb?"

Ah, yes. When, indeed!

✳   ✳   ✳

Once inside the Mirage, we followed the signs directing us to the Psychic Fair and easily found our way to the site at the rear of the hotel. The two ladies seated at the ticket table took our money and handed each of us a large pin-on badge featuring the Psychic Fair logo. It's hard to describe since it was so complicated. Basically, it was a sketch consisting of the planet Earth placed inside of a champagne glass, which was held by a pair of hands with the creases labeled with a palm reader's marks — and all this surrounded by a rainbow of tarot cards and signs of the zodiac. At the bottom, the letters *PF* were written in an intricate, cursive font and looked as if they were etched on the sidewalk by the slime from a couple of wayward snails. Oh, man! What a confused and mixed-up mess that was! Actually, it was kind of funny — a great example of things that are so bad, they're good — like some of those old British "reality shows" on TV that Margaret and I used to watch at our bar down the street from the Ritz.

To say that I was surrounded by The Enemy would be putting it mildly. And that was just from viewing the name tag! What other wicked and ungodly pursuits were awaiting me within? I could hardly wait to find out! After all, it was my *job*!

* * *

As we were pinning those ridiculous badges on our clothes and looking around for the entrance to the actual fair, one of the ladies gave us a nice big fake smile and indicated the large double doors to her right. "Right in there!" she said. "Have a nice time, and don't forget to register for our drawing! We pick a winning number every fifteen minutes, so your chances of winning are extremely good!"

"What do we win? A magic lantern? A flying carpet? *A nose job?*" asked Andy, glancing over at Barbra with an expression of wide-eyed innocence.

A nose job? For Barbra? What does he mean? Could that be true? And then I suddenly recalled his comment, word for word, when he was talking about Barbra's dancing ability a few hours ago. *"It's more like she has it in her genes! Her* mother's *genes. And I don't mean just the dancing part."*

So *that* was it! He was really referring to her *nose job* when he said he didn't mean just the dancing part. Talk about *tit for tat* returning with a vengeance! And here I thought all was forgiven between them with Andy's sweet little apology at the snack shop!

Oh, boy! I wasn't sure how she was going to respond

now, but as it turned out, this time she was way ahead of *me*. In one quick but unobtrusive motion, she raised her hand to adjust the shoulder strap of her purse, and on the way down, her loose fist somehow managed to collide with the most vulnerable part of his body.

"Ooph!" he gasped, definitely *not* joking this time, while Barbra defiantly stood her ground.

"Sorry," she said, her face glowing with a dazzling smile. "Accident."

Holy Bejesus! These kids are barbarians!

"Barbra!" I exclaimed in spite of myself, forgetting my temporary status as a teenager in America and reverting back to my Angelic position of power. "*Bar*bra! That is thoroughly unacceptable!" I grabbed Andy by the arm. "Come on!" I said. "Let's go!"

Still half bent over in pain, he hesitated for a moment before answering. "Uh, no," he groaned. "That's okay. She, well—"

Barbra's brazen smile slowly softened, and she pressed her body up close to his and gently patted his back, and a few seconds later they were both glaring at *me*! I couldn't believe it!

"Well, just don't let it happen again, or I'm *gone*," I threatened. Of course, it was an idle threat. I knew I would never leave her. Besides, I don't know if she even heard me.

The ticket lady — who had been momentarily distracted by a kid who wanted to know where the bathroom was — didn't even have a clue. "Well," she began, resuming our conversation with an indulgent little smile, "we don't have magic lanterns or flying carpets, but we do have several *won*derful prizes, such as coupons for special shows here at the Mirage, as well as autographed books by some of our exhibitors, and also your choice of one of our beautiful stuffed animals! They're something new this year — a Psychic Fair exclusive!"

She indicated the wall behind her, where a menagerie of animals was strung up with varying lengths of elastic string. She smiled and leaned way back in her chair and playfully pulled on the leg of a life-size and realistic-looking green-spotted frog, causing it to flip into the air as if it were alive. "This one is a favorite with the kiddies," she confided, as if it were a big secret.

"Way cool!" said Barbra. "I *want* one of those!"

"Come on," Andy urged. "Let's go in and get this over with."

"*What?*" Barbra asked sharply. "What did you say?"

"I said, let's go in and see what's going on!" He gave her a quick smack on the lips. "It should be great!"

We entered through the double doors, and I was surprised at the size of the room and at the large number of people already milling about. "Wow," Barbra said. "Just *look* at this!"

The exhibitors were stationed in separate booths, which I estimated to be around ninety to one hundred in number. (Approximately ten rows, with eight or ten booths per row. You know me. I did the math!) Each booth was furnished with a couple of chairs and a table, on which were arranged the books, toys, jewelry, or other unholy paraphernalia that the exhibitor was selling. Posters and charts and other such items were tacked on the large dividers along the back and sides of the booths. There were balloons and stuffed animals galore, hanging from the booth dividers as well as from the ceiling above.

I found myself doing the sign of the cross for luck and protection, even though we have no such thing as religious denominations in Heaven. I realize that's a difficult concept for most people to accept, attached and loyal as they are to their own particular brands of Christian worship, but the bickering would be inevitable and constant — with the Catholics criticizing the Anglicans and the Baptists criticizing them both, the Lutherans and Presbyterians having at it, the Greek Orthodox tangling with the Methodists, the Messianic Jews preaching to the Congregationalists, the Mormons standing way off to one side with the Jehovah's Witnesses, and the Unitarians begging to be taken seriously, while the Quakers would be going around trying to make peace with them all. Add to the mix the dozens of small denominations you have never heard of and the din would be intolerable.

Now, as for the other so-called great religions on earth, God may have a separate Heaven for them, but if He has, He hasn't told me about it.

"I think that's where we're supposed to sign up for the drawing," Andy remarked, indicating a table just to the left of the door. A slightly overweight and pink-cheeked gentleman wearing a bow tie was sitting at a computer, popping pretzels into his mouth — which, somehow, brought to my mind a certain hungry baby bird chirping in his nest that I once saw at *Le Jardin des Tuileries*. The little birdie was straining his whole body upward with his mouth wide open, waiting for the fat worm dangling from his mother's beak. *Oh, Lordy! I do miss Paris so much!*

Andy grabbed Barbra's hand. "Come on. Let's sign up. I'll win you that stuffed animal you want. I'm feeling very lucky today, amid all these good vibes." Then he motioned to me with a toss of his head. "Come on. You, too. They pick a winning number every fifteen minutes, you know, so your chances of winning are *extremely* good!" I detected some more sarcasm there, but I went along with him anyway.

The gentleman at the computer put aside his bag of pretzels and welcomed us warmly with a cheerful "Howdy!"

"You go first," Andy said to Barbra, giving her a little push, while I stood a few feet away, looking over the scene, trying to spot the infamous Dr. Stanley J. Featherstone, author of that bordering-on-the-blasphemous book *Guardian Angels: Our Friends in Need.* I couldn't wait for a chance to get over to his booth and set him straight about the pitiful and fallacious claim that deceased humans — most often children — can become God's Special Angels in Heaven, equipped with wings, a halo, and a helpful spirit.

Suddenly I heard Andy call out to me, "Hey, Noah! It's your turn. Come on."

I stepped up to the man at the computer.

"Your name, please?"

"Uh, Noah."

"And your last name, Noah?"

Oh, jeez! I don't know *my last name. If only I had taken time to read my driver's license when I had the chance! Angel Jake! Angel Jake! Help!*

He repeated the question. "And your last name, my friend?"

"Do you really *need* that?"

"Yes, I do, if you want to enter the drawing. Your last name, and your address as well, please."

Barbra and Andy were still standing there just a few feet away, waiting for me. She was examining the stuffed animals on display at an adjoining table, and Andy was fiddling around with his cell phone. As I think back on it now, I should have just made up something and let it go at that. I could have easily said Dumas or Chirac, or even Dior or Flaubert, but to tell you the truth, it just never occurred to me to lie about it. Instead, I did something really stupid. I confronted the poor guy with a preposterous challenge.

"Why don't you tell *me*? This *is* the Psychic Fair, isn't it? You guys are supposed to have extraordinary powers that allow you to see into the future and beyond the physical world — in other words, *God's* powers. So why don't you think about it real hard and then *you* tell *me* what my last name is?"

The man blushed a bright red and stuck a couple of fingers under his shirt collar and scratched his neck. "I'm sorry," he replied. "But I'm not a psychic. I just work here."

Again, how easy it would have been to simply make up a name! But suddenly, it was too late, because there was Andy, right in my face. "What's wrong? What's holding us up?"

The man at the computer and I exchanged glances. Then we both spoke at once.

"He won't give me his last name."

"He wants to know my last name."

Andy squinted at me. "So tell him already!"

"What if I don't want to? What if they start sending me a bunch of pornographic junk mail, or salesmen come knocking at my door, asking me to buy encyclopedias or magazine subscriptions or vacuum cleaners?"

"That definitely won't happen, sir!" the man said indignantly. "We don't give out this information to anyone!"

"For God's sake, tell him your name, Noah," Barbra chimed in. "There's a certain person here I wish to speak with before she leaves, so will you please hurry up?"

I still didn't answer. What could I say? I mean, put yourself in my place. What would *you* have done? Talk about being between a rock and a hard place! Now I know what it feels like!

Andy leaned over the table. "Sark," he said. "His name is Noah Sark." Then he looked at me. "Now tell the nice man your address and let's get moving."

Noah Sark? Noah's Ark! *Oh, no! I don't believe it! Wait till I get back! Just* wait *until I get back!*

The man at the computer smiled at me — but it was really more of a smirk. "Your address, Mr. Sark?"

Of course, I didn't know my address either! I just barely got a glimpse at my driver's license, for crying out loud! Angels Camp, California. That's the extent of it. That's all I knew. Ah, but I had *learned* from my mistake. I simply made something up.

"Three thirty-three Tuileries Lane, Angels Camp, California."

The man looked up at me, hands poised on the computer keys. "What's that again? I didn't quite get the street name."

"Tuileries! *Tuileries!* It's the French word for tiles. As in *Le Jardin des Tuileries!*" *Doesn't this guy know* anything? *What a bozo.*

He slid a piece of paper over to me. "Will you please write it down?"

Then ol' Andy butted in again. "Did you move or something?"

"Huh?" I finished writing on the slip of paper and started to slide it back to the man.

But Andy intercepted it with a deft movement of his own hand and quickly scanned what I had written. "Your driver's license — I remember it said you lived on some number street. Fifteenth or Sixteenth, something like that. So did you move?"

Uh-oh. Possible snag here. Better play it cool. "Oh, yeah, that's right. I did. I just haven't had a chance to change it yet. Thanks for reminding me, though. I'll fix that when I get back home."

"Right," said Andy, looking me straight in the eye in a way that kind of scared me, it was so searching and intense — as if he could see right through me, actually. "Yes." He nodded. "You'd better do that."

The three of us stayed together for a few minutes, strolling down Aisle A and stopping briefly at every booth. Barbra was the first to go off on her own. "You guys are moving too slow for me," she said. "I'm going to go look for Gloria-Marie. I'll meet up with you later."

Andy and I remained together for the next couple of booths, just idly strolling along, making various comments as we went. Pretty soon he stopped to tie his shoe, and when he stood up again, he asked me a question from out of the blue.

"Listen," he said. "I don't suppose you've had a chance to contact Jeff yet today, have you? I mean, we've been together most of the time and I didn't notice you on the phone —"

"Jeff?"

Andy leaned forward, his eyes looking directly into mine. "Yeah. You know. Your friend Jeff, the guy who borrowed your car?"

"Oh!" I exclaimed. "You mean *that* Jeff!"

Boy, let me tell you! That's the trouble with making things up. You've really got to be on your toes every minute. This particular lapse was probably not that important, but still.

"Yes," he assured me. "*That* Jeff. Does he still have your car, or what?"

I sighed and shook my head. "I'm sure he does. He

said he'd like to borrow it all weekend. I think he said he wanted to impress a girl or something." *Uh-oh. There I go again. I'd better remember that. Trying to impress a girl.*

Andy's expression softened. He shoved his hands in his pockets and kind of bounced up and down on his heels, as if something had just occurred to him. "Well, I remember you said that you didn't feel too welcome at his house last night, with him not around and all, so maybe you want to crash over at my place tonight. I should check with my mom first," he said. "But I'm sure it'll be okay."

Wow! Did I hear him right? I guess that means we're really friends! "Well, uh — gosh," I stammered. "That'd be great." *Praise the Lord! No Dumpster for me this time!*

"Good," he said. "That's settled."

We were standing in front of a booth featuring a Holistic Massage by Vickie, according to the large sign hanging above it. Vickie happened to be a very attractive young woman dressed in bright red shorts and a brief halter top. A large poster on the back wall of her booth enumerated the many advantages of Holistic Massage, including Personal Healing, Transforming Your Life, The Ability to Push Your Limits, Finding Spiritual Growth, Peace of Mind, and Discovering Financial Success.

People were queued up, waiting for their free trial massage. "Listen," said Andy, checking his watch. "I think I might want to take Vickie up on that free offer of hers. You know, give it a try, since we're here." He pressed his fingers against the corners of his mouth to keep himself from smiling. "Uh, why don't you go on without me and I'll catch up to you later."

"Sure," I said. "There's someone here I want to see myself."

Andy was no sooner in line than bells started to ring and drums started to beat and the room lights started to blink off and on. "Attention! Attention!" came a loud voice echoing throughout the hall. "It's time again for another Psychic Fair drawing!"

Everything stopped cold. Even Andy's masseuse stood idle. Every eye was focused on the small stage set up at the front of the room. A tall, thin woman dressed in some kind of mysterious sari-looking gown read from an elaborate scroll in her hand.

"Here are the lucky winners of the second drawing for this hour!" she announced. Then she read off three names, pausing slightly between them. "Will the lucky winners please come up and claim your prizes!

And remember, if you didn't win this time, there will be another drawing in fifteen short minutes!"

Just like magic, the room suddenly came to life again. I gave Andy a little wave and started on my hunt for Dr. Stanley J. Featherstone. But first I had to duck out into the hallway for a quick smoke.

CHAPTER SEVENTEEN

I RECOGNIZED DR. FEATHERSTONE right away from his photo on the back of his book. However, I'm sorry to say that he didn't resemble his picture all that much. His mustache was bushier now, and he had lost some hair and gained some wrinkles. He was standing by a table stacked high with his books, earnestly chatting with a young mother holding a toddler by the hand.

Seeing his books there on the table gave me a great idea. Why not present my own copy of his book to him as if I were about to ask him to autograph it, but instead, once I had his attention, really sock it to him! Perfect! I had several passages of the Bible on the tip of my tongue that I could quote for him, of course, detailing the circumstances of God's creation of his Heavenly Host, and then I could chastise him quite severely for misstating the facts as he did in his book.

I stepped out of the aisle and stood against the wall while I slipped off my rucksack and fished out the book. Then, putting on my best innocent expression, I approached his booth and stood silently next to the woman with the toddler.

Of course, I couldn't avoid hearing their conversation. The woman was obviously upset, and she kept dabbing at her eyes with a wad of soggy tissues.

"I was so happy to get a chance to speak with you this afternoon, Dr. Featherstone," she was saying. "And I just can't *tell* you how much — how *very* much — your book has helped me."

Dr. Featherstone reached out and patted her lightly on her shoulder, and she immediately reacted to that show of tenderness by bowing her head and quietly starting to sob. The little girl standing at her side looked up at her mother with such a pained and frightened expression that it was all I could do to keep from bending down and comforting the child myself.

The woman was struggling to speak. "Just knowing

for *certain* that our darling little Cindy is in Heaven was a great comfort to us, of course, but —"

"Mommy!" the little girl suddenly cried out. "Pick up! Mommy, pick up!"

Dr. Featherstone immediately reached down and picked up the little girl and handed her into her mother's arms. The woman kissed the back of the child's head and tried to smile, in spite of her trembling lips.

"Where Thindy, where Thindy?" the little girl lisped, tears flooding her own eyes.

"They were twins, you see, my precious Susie here and little Cindy, and they were so close —"

"Let me assure you again, my dear," said Dr. Featherstone. "Cindy is *indeed* one of God's Special Angels, and she always will be." He hesitated slightly, just for a fleeting moment, and then turned and started to sift through several piles of the books that were stacked on his table.

"Oh! Here we go," he said, holding a small book in his hand and smiling benevolently. "I have a new picture book for toddlers out this year." He handed the book to little Susie. "There are two editions, actually. One to help young siblings cope with the loss of sisters, and one for brothers."

I caught a glimpse of the cover — and winced. It was a picture of a very beautiful Angel-child of an indeterminate age. She had atrocious wings, of course, but a quite genuine-looking halo, if I do say so myself. (Most of the time, the halos I see on earth art are so *wrong* it's laughable.)

"The book usually sells for eight ninety-five," Dr. Featherstone was saying, "but I wish you would accept this copy with my compliments."

While the woman was struggling for words, Dr. Featherstone took his eyes off her for a moment and looked directly into mine. "Yes?" he asked gently, noticing the book in my hand. "Would you like me to autograph that for you?"

Little Susie was clumsily turning the thick pages of her book. "Thindy God's Angel now," she whispered to herself, with her chubby little cheeks puffing up into a sweet baby smile.

Dr. Featherstone's question hung in the air. I swallowed, and swallowed again. "Yes," I said finally. "If you would, please."

I know. I know. Just call me Mr. Wimp. But hey — what would *you* do?

✳   ✳   ✳

Oh, no! Once again I had forgotten my sacred duty. Not only had I lost sight of Barbra, I also had no idea where she was or if she was in trouble. But wait! I *did* know where she was! Where else but at the booth of a certain Gloria-Marie! So see? I'm not as incompetent as I thought I was!

I figured that my best bet would be to climb onto the small stage and hope that I'd be able to pinpoint her from that higher vantage point. I spotted Andy first, however. He was standing in a quiet spot over by the windows, talking very intently on his cell. His head was bowed and he was looking down at the floor, his free hand gesturing impatiently with short jabs into the air. I couldn't take my eyes off him. What could be so important? And then, suddenly, he stopped speaking and gesturing and just stood there tapping his foot, but still holding the phone up to his ear. After two or three minutes, he once again became animated, but he seemed to have gotten his way. By the time he hooked the phone back on his belt, even the most amateurish psychic in the room would be able to discern that he was extremely pleased with himself.

Gloria-Marie's booth was quite unique. Instead of a large table and one or two chairs, it had five folding chairs arranged in a semicircle around a portable plastic countertop. Gloria-Marie's chair was on the opposite side of the counter from the folding chairs. It was one of those high-backed, upholstered jobs with wooden armrests and a little open space between the back and the seat. I remember seeing chairs like that at an antique store with the Princess, and if I'm not mistaken, the style is called a French Throne Chair. But Gloria-Marie's was really a dilly, with its psychedelic print of gold, red, black, and silver and carved armrests.

All five of the visitors' chairs were occupied, with Barbra sitting in the center. Next to her, on her right, was a timid-looking fellow wearing a light gray sport coat with the sleeves a couple of inches too short, and beside him, on the end, was a young woman dressed in white shorts and a *Star Trek* T-shirt. On Barbra's left were a middle-aged woman and her young son, a real, genuine American brat, around seven or eight years old. I can state that fact unequivocally — not because of my Angelic Insight this time, but because I had a chance to observe him in action while I was having my cigarette break in the hallway. The main bone of contention between him and his mother was his official Psychic Fair stuffed frog, which he was utilizing variously as a weapon, a fan, a crawling monster, a flying zombie, a rocket ship, a bandit, a hat, and a whirling dervish — which (as you are probably aware) is a member of a curious religious sect about which I have absolutely nothing to say at this time.

After a good scolding and mild shaking, the mother, for some inexplicable reason, allowed the child to maintain possession of his Psychic Fair frog. And now, there he was, sitting next to Barbra and demonstrating his complete repertoire, both *for* her and *to* her.

I was standing in the aisle in front of the booth, watching all of this from a few feet away, when I suddenly felt that familiar whack on the side of my head — my first attack since I had spotted Barbra sitting at the table by the window at Angelo's that morning.

What is the meaning of this? What am I to do? Oh, think, Noah, think! Or, rather, don't think! Just let it flow, let it flow. Let the picture form in your mind from the random dust of possibilities. I closed my eyes and opened myself up to the flow. What was that I envisioned? Oh, Heavens! What could it be? The Holy Grail? The Sacred Chalice? No, no. It was neither of those. The Star of Bethlehem, shining so brightly o'er the humble shepherds on that glorious night? No. It was not the Star. In fact, it was nothing like the Star! *Ah! There it is! Coming into view now, as clear as day. It's the frog! It's the dead green-spotted frog currently residing in the thirty-two-ounce soft-drink cup in my rucksack!* Oh, I knew there must be a reason for that! And now, at last, its time had come!

I turned my back, slipped off my rucksack, and quickly removed the cold-drink container, first swiping at it haphazardly with the pair of shorts that was wrapped around it. Then I hurriedly slipped my pack over one shoulder and held the container in my hand as if it were, indeed, a nice cold drink just waiting to be enjoyed.

The timid man in the sport coat was now shaking hands with Gloria-Marie. He stood up and awkwardly bowed to the others, then hurriedly walked away from the group. That's when Gloria-Marie beckoned to me. "Would you care to join us?" she called out as Barbra turned and smiled at me, raising her hand and signaling for me to do just that. But as I approached and was starting to take the vacated seat next to her, Barbra suddenly slid under me in a graceful ballet movement that appeared to this rank amateur to be a combination of a *grand plié* and a *glissade*, and sat there herself, leaving me no alternative other than occupying the chair beside the little hellion with the stuffed frog.

As soon as I was seated, Gloria-Marie closed her

heavily mascaraed eyes and took a deep, long breath, letting her head fall back as if she were smelling the storied ambrosia of the mythical gods erroneously worshipped long ago by the clueless citizens of Rome and Greece. Then she slowly opened her eyes and gazed benevolently upon each of us in turn, whispering ever so mysteriously, "Oh, people — I feel the *magic* all around me! Something very wonderful and magical has happened during this session! Can't you feel it, too?"

Barbra and the others all nodded in agreement, except for the little demon sitting at my side. All he did was give me a good pummeling on the head with his green stuffed frog, and then he burst out laughing like the very Devil himself.

"Donny!" exclaimed his mother. "Stop that *right now!*" She grabbed the frog from his hand and placed it out of his reach — up toward the far edge of the counter and way over on my territory. "If you touch that *one more time,*" she threatened, "I will not be responsible for what happens to it!"

Gloria-Marie suddenly stiffened and gave the child a cold and stony look that even had me scared. "And neither will *I*, young man," she said. She continued to stare at him until he finally blinked first. Then she turned to us again. "I'm going to take a bit of a break now," purred Gloria-Marie, rising from her chair. "And when I return, we will quickly review the valuable insights we have gained about ourselves, and what we can do with them to make our lives more happy and fulfilling in every way."

Barbra waited until Gloria-Marie was out of earshot, and then she grabbed my arm and gave it a little shake. "Oh, Noah! She was *so great*! She told me that I should return the rocks, and that as soon as I do that, my mother's grip on me would be loosened forever! I would be *free*!"

"Gosh, that *is* great," I said, halfway understanding what she meant about her *mother's grip on her* but completely in the dark about the *returning the rocks* part.

Out of the corner of my eye, I suddenly caught sight of Donny slyly reaching out and actually touching the frog, in spite of the dire warnings still echoing in the air around us. *What a little creep!* I nudged him with my elbow and pointed my finger at him as if it were a loaded pistol. *Now where did I learn to do that?* I thought, as the kid scowled back at me. But he *did* withdraw his hand.

"But still," Barbra was saying, "I'm just not *sure* about her. I mean, you heard her say that something wonderful and magical has happened this session? But still, I haven't seen any real evidence of that — yet."

"Well, what did she say you should do? And what's this thing with *the rocks,* anyway?"

Barbra leaned toward me and spoke so fast I could hardly keep up with her. "Remember when I told you at lunch how my mom announced to my dad and me that she got the part in *Hello, Dolly!* while the three of us were vacationing in Death Valley? Well, she also told us that she was moving to New York City and didn't know how long she would be there."

"Oh, gee," I said. "That must have been pretty devastating."

"Well, after she told us that, I got this crazy idea that if I took a couple of the rocks that were all around there and kept them with me, somehow they would make her come back home to us. As long as I *kept* the rocks, you see?" She paused, then added, "You know how kids are, always imagining things like that?"

I nodded again, even though I *didn't* know what she meant, since I can't recall ever being a kid.

"But then," she went on, "while we were walking back to the car, I saw this big sign that said it was unlawful to remove *anything* from Death Valley, since it's a National Monument, and therefore had special protection. But I just ignored the sign. Something made me take the rocks home anyway."

She quickly reached inside her purse and pulled out a small plastic bag. I could see that it held several reddish-colored rocks, and also some bits of sand and dirt.

"Here they are," she said. "I always have them with me. But what Gloria-Marie just told me was that I shouldn't have taken them in the first place, and it was *the rocks* that were keeping me from facing the fact that my mother will never come back." She paused to take a breath. "But the good part is that I don't think it actually matters anymore! I don't think I *need* her anymore!"

I impulsively grabbed her hand and gave it a little squeeze. "That's great!" I said. "So what's the problem? Just take the rocks back, and that will be the end of it."

"But there *is* a problem," she said quietly. "How can I trust her? Gloria-Marie, I mean. Did she *really* sense something magical about our session? To hear Andy talk, all this psychic business is, in his words, just a bunch of hooey. We've had some pretty nasty arguments about that."

I couldn't think of how to respond to her. Actually,

it was more than just a bunch of hooey. It was downright dangerous!

"What if I had the right idea about the rocks in the first place?" Barbra went on. "Maybe, if I hang on to them, she *will* come back home." She paused again, and a funny little smile appeared on her face. "Maybe she'll lose her singing voice, or get sick or something —" The smile disappeared, and for a moment I thought she might start crying. "Oh, just listen to me! Did I actually say that?"

But then, all of a sudden, it happened again: The drums started to beat and the bells started to ring. Off and on went the lights, and over the loudspeakers came the announcement. "Attention! Attention! It's time for another Psychic Fair drawing!" All eyes were once again glued to the stage. Even those of Demon Donny, sitting alongside me.

Now! something told me. *Do it now!*

So I did. Like a perfectly coordinated and well-greased machine in a modern bottling plant, with one hand I quickly flipped off the lid from my soft-drink cup and pulled out the deceased frog, while the other hand unobtrusively reached out and swept the stuffed frog into the newly vacated space. Then I quickly replaced the lid on my container, pushed the corpse with my elbow to a prominent position directly in front of my little adversary, and waited for the inevitable.

It came just a few seconds later. The kid didn't exactly scream. It was more like the sound of — well, I can't say exactly *what* it was like the sound of. It might make you ill. Let me just say it was something like a long, drawn-out *choking* sound — like choking on a horse, for instance. Actually, it was a *beautiful* sound. And then the kid just upped and ran! He slid off his chair so fast that he stumbled to his knees, but he quickly picked himself up again and charged off down the aisle like a souped-up Bugatti being chased by *la police française* on the road to La Baule, which, I might add, can be very fast indeed.

To say the least, Donny's mom was somewhat taken aback at this turn of events. Actually, she was stunned. Bug-eyed and whitefaced, she glanced first one way and then another, saw the dead frog, and immediately took off after Donny, calling out, "Donny! *Donny!* Wait for me!"

"Jeez! What happened to *them*?" Barbra exclaimed, watching Donny's mother chasing after the kid lickety-split down the aisle.

And then she spotted the frog. "*Yuck!* Is that a dead frog, or what?" She reached over to poke it, but then suddenly withdrew her hand. "It *is* a dead frog. How did *that* get there?"

"Darned if I know!"

"Did that kid do it? "

"I don't think so! I think he just saw it there and took off."

There was a long, hushed silence. I watched as Barbra's expression changed from simple surprise to awe and wonderment. It was amazing to behold. "I just don't get it," she mused. She thought a minute or so and then added, "But Gloria-Marie *did* mention the word *magic*, didn't she? Didn't she say that something wonderful and magical has happened this session? She must have meant *something* by that."

Next, Barbra had a question for me, but she phrased it like a statement. "I don't suppose that *you* had anything to do with it —"

"Me?" I tried to look both innocent and surprised. "How could I?"

(I must interrupt my narrative again here to forewarn you that answering a question with a question — in a situation such as that — is not, technically, considered to be a lie. Except when you are evaluated on Judgment Day, and your *real* intentions are finally taken into consideration. So take heed, and be very, very careful when you tread upon that treacherous ground.)

"Okay! That *settles* it!" Barbra hopped off her chair. "No need to wait for Gloria-Marie! I'll just send her an e-mail later. Right now I have to find Andy and persuade him to drive me to Death Valley! The sooner the better!" She dropped the little bag with the rocks back into her purse and grabbed my hand. "Hey!" she said. "Do you want to come along? It might be fun!"

I pretended to think about it for a minute, while an unexpected voice inside my head sang out in spite of myself, *"O my sweet! Wither you go I will follow."*

Stop that! I told myself. *That is not right, and you know it!* Then I smiled at her and said as calmly as I could, "Sure. I'd really like that."

We left the booth to start searching for Andy, and on our way I slipped my thirty-two-ounce soft-drink container into the trash can located at the end of the aisle. It made quite a clunk, but no one appeared to notice.

chapter eighteen

WE FOUND ANDY SITTING on the floor by the double doors where we had come in, his arms dangling over his bent knees and a very bored look on his face. He quickly checked his watch when he saw us approaching and I expected him to ask what took us so long, but Barbra didn't give him a chance.

She hurried over to him and offered her hand to help boost him up on his feet. "Oh, *man!*" she said, before he could open his mouth. "You'll never believe what just happened!"

"Probably not. What was it?"

"I'll tell you in a minute. But first, can I ask you a question?"

Andy cocked his head to the side and gave her a one-eyed squint. "Hmm. Let me see. The question you're asking me is, *could* you ask me a question. Right?"

Barbra looked both annoyed and impatient. "Uh, yeah. I guess so."

"Well, you just *asked* me a question without first asking if you could! How do you explain that? How come you didn't *ask* me if you could *ask* me if you could ask me a question?"

"What? What are you talking about?"

Andy just stood there, grinning at her. Actually, I thought it was really mean of him to tease her like that when it was so obvious that she wanted to talk to him about something urgent.

But she soon caught on to his little joke, if you could call it that. "Oh, *you*!" she said, suddenly reaching up and giving his hair a good tousling. I found myself sort of wishing she'd do that to me, until I remembered my wig. And then I was glad she didn't.

"Okay then, here's the *real* question," she said. "How would you like to do me a big fat favor and drive me over to Death Valley this afternoon?"

"Death Valley? This afternoon? It's a couple of hours away, sweetie." He glanced at me, as if he were waiting for me to fill him in on the details. But when I just shrugged, he asked her himself. "What *for?*"

Naturally, she had to explain the whole story to him then, about the rocks and all — and how Gloria-Marie had convinced her what she must do in order to "free herself forever from the painful and impossible dream of someday capturing her mother's love."

At first, Andy made no secret of the fact that he was more than a little skeptical of Gloria-Marie's solution, voicing his opinion of her in three short words: "What a kook."

And as far as the dead-frog incident was concerned — well, he simply refused to take it seriously. In fact, he thought it was really funny. A trick, for sure, but a really funny one. I guess, under the circumstances, I had to agree with him.

I didn't expect him to even *consider* driving Barbra so far for what he called "an inane reason," so it really shocked me to hear him say that maybe he *could* do it, after all. "Death Valley, huh? Hmm. That just might work out."

"*Really?*" Barbra exclaimed, obviously just as surprised as I was that she didn't have to spend more time trying to talk him into it.

He thought about it some more, and then he began to nod. "You know," he repeated, "that just might work out. But not until tomorrow. And I'll have to make a few phone calls first." He paused a moment, then nudged me with his elbow. "Hey, Noah. I don't suppose you've ever seen a genuine royal white tiger roaming around in Angels Camp, have you?"

What a strange question. What's he getting at? "I don't think so. No. I'm pretty sure I haven't."

He grabbed Barbra's hand. "Let's take him over to see the tigers. You two can entertain them while I make my calls."

They led me to a beautiful open-air space called the White Tiger Habitat — still within the Mirage Hotel complex — but complete with a gorgeous swimming pool and fountains and fake mountains. Behind a slanted glass barrier, minding their own business, were two very spectacular but haughty white tigers with black stripes and very, very sinister blue eyes.

"I'll be right over there," Andy said, pointing. "Over by that bench across the way."

Barbra waved him off. Then she took my arm and moved up close to the glass. "I haven't been here in a long time," she whispered. "Aren't they beautiful?"

I nodded. "Yes, they are. Very proud, and powerful, too."

"You know," she confided, "sometimes I can't help believing that they *really* wouldn't hurt me if I just slowly walked up to them and curled up between their front legs and gave them a hug around the neck. Especially that big male there. I've always wanted to wrap my arms around him and nuzzle up to him ever since the first time I saw him."

She suddenly grabbed onto my arm. "Look at him! He's staring right at me — like he's inviting me in! Oh, God! He's so *sweet!*"

She let go of my arm and took a few tentative steps around to her right, kind of peering toward the back of the glass enclosure. "Hmm. I wonder where the door to that enclosure is. How do they get those guys in and out of there, anyway?"

I guess I went a little overboard then. But don't you see? I had *no idea* what awful tragedy might be in store for her. How could I know whether it might be a tiger, tearing her to bits right in front of my eyes? I just couldn't afford to take chances. So I did what I had to do. Faster than you could say *Aéroport Charles de Gaulle,* I made a lunge for her, grabbing her around her waist and halting her in her tracks. The sudden force of my body against hers knocked both of us slightly off balance, but not to the floor, thank goodness.

"Noah! My *God!* What are you *doing?*" she gasped. But at least she didn't scream.

"I — I don't know," I stammered. "Sometimes I just get the awful feeling that you're in trouble, and I need to —" I shrugged, unable to finish my sentence.

She reared back on the heels of her little white boots and stared at me, wide-eyed — and by the look on her face, perhaps even momentarily unhinged. "You know something, Noah? Sometimes I get the feeling that you might be my Guardian Angel in disguise — the way you've been hovering over me ever since we first met this morning."

I could feel the blood suddenly draining from my face and my brain going completely blank. There was no way I could respond to that.

But Barbra herself broke the spell. "I guess it's that hair of yours," she said with a laugh. "Hey, I've gotten along just fine all these years without a Guardian Angel. Why would I need one now?"

Whew! That was close! If she found out the truth — well, if you ask me, I couldn't tell you what might happen if she found out the truth. The only place I know of that actually happening is in the Bible! Anyway, for me at least, the crisis is over for now.

"Hey, where'd that Andy go?" I asked, purposely changing the subject.

"Over there," she said, pointing at him. "He's still on the phone. Let's go find out what's happening."

I thought it was odd that Andy would turn away from us and shield his mouth with his free hand as we walked up to him. But I caught a couple fragments of his conversation anyway. He was talking with his father, because he said something like "I'm sure of it, Pop," and "How about tomorrow?" And then I heard him say in a softer voice, "Well, they said it could be touchy — they don't want to shock him —" When he saw me there so close to him, he gave me a tight little smile and nonverbally indicated that he was trying to get off the phone as quickly as he could. But he still turned away while he finished his conversation.

He clipped his cell to his trousers and came over to me, acting quite worried and concerned. "It's my dog," he explained, shoving his hands in his pockets and avoiding my eyes. "He's at the vet, and he's scheduled to have surgery in a couple of days . . ." His voice drifted off. "I'm pretty worried about him."

"Oh, I'm sorry —"

"Ah, that reminds me," he said. "I'd better check with my mom about tonight."

He whipped out his cell and quickly punched in a number. She answered right away, and he sure didn't waste words. But they weren't the ones I was expecting. "Mom? Hi. Did Pop call you yet?"

Barbra and I just stood there, listening, but only because we couldn't avoid it.

"Yeah? Did he say anything about tomorrow?" Slight pause. "No, it's okay. I already talked with Uncle Buck." Another pause. "Oh, one more thing. Well, two, actually. First, can I borrow your car in the morning?" He nodded. "Great. And is it okay if Noah spends the night? You know, it's —" He continued to nod. "Perfect!" He grinned and gave me the thumbs-up sign. "Thanks, Mom. See you later then. Oh, and don't wait up for us. We may be in pretty late."

He flipped shut his cell and put it away. "I think we're all set." But then he suddenly turned to Barbra. "Oh — jeez! I forgot to ask *you.* Do you have any plans yet for tomorrow? I mean, is your father expecting you or anything —?"

"Hey, I'm free as the breeze," she broke in. "Remember, I told you that on the day we met?"

Then she flashed me a quick but bitter smile. You must know the kind of smile I mean — the kind that isn't really a smile at all, just a half-second facsimile of one that dissolves before it even takes hold.

"There *are* certain advantages to *not* having a mother around, and with a father involved in showbiz," she explained, looking away. "You get to do pretty much as you please."

A few seconds passed before Andy broke the silence.

"Okay!" he said brightly, taking Barbra's hand. "Noah and I will pick you up at your place at seven in the morning, and then we'll drive right over to the airport."

"The *airport*?" Barbra and I exclaimed in unison. Barbra laughed at that, but I didn't see anything funny about it at all. In fact, it scared me to death.

"Did I miss something?" I asked. "Did you say *airport*?"

Andy laughed and clapped me on the shoulder. "Oh, just a little surprise I've cooked up for you guys. Hey, I'll bet neither one of you has ever been up for a joyride in a brand-new Cessna 182!"

A private plane! Oh, no! Just what I need! This has to be the moment I've been dreading. Jake! Oh, Jake! Come on! What if there's a problem while we're up there? You know I can't perform that kind of miraculous miracle anymore! Those days are gone forever, remember? But oh, how I still long for those olden days of yore, back in Biblical Times, or the Middle Ages, or even the Early Renaissance, when life was so much easier for us Guardian Angels! Miracles were still happening all over the place like clockwork, simply because no one knew how to disprove them. Maintaining a pure and innocent faith in those days was as easy as pie. But it's a different story now. With all your advances in science and technology, plus the growing boldness of those shortsighted and foolhardy skeptics among you, pulling off a genuine miracle is no longer such an easy task. There is always someone to dispute it, some expert to investigate the origin of the Madonna's tears, or to ask permission to view the before and after X-rays of the miraculously cured patient. And *please*, don't even get me started on those relentlessly pesky guys from CSI — the so-called Committee for Skeptical Inquiry. You'd laugh your heads off if you could hear ol' Angel Jake rake *them* over the coals! Ah, yes. In these Latter Days it takes both strength *and* courage, and even a touch of nobility to toss reason to the winds and proclaim with conviction and verve, *I believe.*

I was awakened from my short trip down memory lane by the sound of Barbra's happy little yelp. "Oh!" she exclaimed, jumping up and down like a five-year-old. "I've always wanted to go up in a private plane!"

"Great," said Andy, grinning at her. "I had a hunch

you'd go for it. My uncle Buck is plotting our course now. He didn't promise that he'd take you directly *over* Badwater, but he's sure we'll be flying near there — at least over the territory marked National Monument on his map."

"That's good enough!" Barbra said. She reached over and threw her arms around his neck. And then she gave him a big kiss — on the lips, I might add. I couldn't tell if I was jealous or embarrassed, but it was probably a combination of both. What a lucky guy!

"But wait!" I interjected. "Is it *legal* to drop things from airplanes? Like *rocks,* for instance. That *can't* be legal, can it?"

"Oh, no! It's *fine.* No *problemo!*" Andy said while Barbra just looked at me and rolled her eyes.

Andy extended his arms outward in a slow, luxurious stretch, and then brought his hands up to the top of his shoulders and raised his elbows high into the air. "Whew!" he breathed, relaxing again and checking his watch. "It's, uh — let's see — just four o'clock." He happened to be standing between me and Barbra, and he put his arms around our shoulders and pulled us together in a close little circle, the same way he did back at Angelo's. "It's almost four o'clock," he repeated, "and we've got all evening ahead of us. So what do you guys want to do?"

chapter nineteen

I DIDN'T REALIZE THAT BEING ON EARTH could be so much fun until I spent those few magic hours with my new friends on the fabulous Las Vegas Strip. At last I was finally able to understand why human beings are sometimes so reluctant to leave this sorry and sinful abode for the divine sublimity of Heaven. But now I know. Once they have experienced such a wonderfully lovely time on earth as I spent last night, they never lose the desire and longing for the chance to relive even just a part of the joy of those glorious hours once again. Ah, I know what you're probably thinking, and I'm sorry to disappoint you, but sex had nothing to do with it. The real joy was experiencing true and sincere bonding with my two fabulous new friends in the most magical and illusory town in all of WackiWorld — Las Vegas, Nevada.

We exited the Mirage just in time to witness the spectacular Eruption of the Volcano — an earsplitting event that happens on the Strip once an hour on the hour, with a possibility of more frequent eruptions during the busier tourist seasons, according to the explanation given to me afterward by my two knowledgeable guides.

"Whoa!" I shouted at the sound of the first rumblings. "What's going on?"

"It's the volcano," Barbra said, cupping her hands around her mouth so I might hear her better. "It's getting ready to blow. Here," she said, grabbing my hand. "Quick. Follow me!" She pulled me through the growing throng of tourists until we were pushed up right against the railing with an unobstructed view of the rising mountain in front of us.

At that moment nothing could seem more real, even though somewhere in the recesses of my mind I must have known it was all a show — a multimillion-dollar technological masterpiece in the art of make-believe.

I squeezed Barbra's hand, and when she squeezed mine back, it was like an answer to a prayer.

"Look! It's really picking up steam now!" she shouted.

And so I watched, spellbound, as the eruption built up stage by stage to a final stirring crescendo, with huge colored streams of red and purple molten lava shooting up into the sky and then dropping down again, spilling over the rim, accompanied by perfectly orchestrated sound effects and soaring music to complete the spectacle. I suddenly found myself praising God for the priceless Gift of Optimism that He has bestowed upon all mankind. What trait other than Optimism could coax from otherwise rational human beings the odds-defying gambling dollars needed to fund that amazing display?

When it was over, we found Andy waiting for us at the edge of the crowd.

"So what did you think of that?" he asked, his face strangely aglow. "Pretty amazing, huh?"

I had to laugh at the two of them — standing there as if they themselves were responsible for the whole thing.

"Hey," I remarked with what I hoped was an accusingly humorous grin, "I thought you guys said you didn't notice that stuff anymore."

They exchanged sheepish looks, but Barbra answered

for them both. "We don't!" she said, and we all began to laugh.

We walked a short distance to the next attraction — the actual sinking of a Pirate Ship into a huge expanse of water, including the Real-Live Pirates and Ladies of the Night that were aboard the ship. The enchanting entrance to the Treasure Island Hotel and Casino beckoned just beyond the water.

"It's so much fun having you here!" Barbra shouted as we were squeezed like sardines within the good-natured crowd watching from the sidewalk. "It's like seeing all this for the first time all over again!" She pounded on Andy's shoulder to get his attention. "Isn't that right?"

I'm not exactly sure that he understood or even heard her question, but, nevertheless, he grinned and shouted back, "Yeah! That's right!"

Later, after admiring the campily fake replicas of the Rialto Bridge, the Doge's Palace, and the famous Campanile in Saint Mark's Square, impossibly situated adjacent to each other like a bad Picasso dream, we ventured inside the Venetian Hotel to experience even more of Venice. Barbra wanted to ride on the gondola down the little fake canal, so we did, singing and swaying to the tune of "That's Amore," accompanied by an ever-smiling accordion player seated in front of the gondolier. Even *he* broke up when Andy starting singing his own version of the song. Instead of the original words, he sang:

> *When the moon hits the sky*
> *With a big piece of pie,*
> *Catch some-more hay.*

Later, as the gondolier was helping us out of the boat, Barbra laughed and said, "I can't believe I actually went on that ride!" Then she added with an exaggerated frown, "Oh, nuts! You know what *that* means! Now I can't make fun of it anymore!"

The young guy disguised as a gondolier raised his hands helplessly and smiled apologetically as if he knew the feeling exactly.

We ambled down the Strip from one end to the other, gawking at huge fish tanks and million-dollar chandeliers, applauding the free circus acts high up in the big top at Circus Circus, admiring the pyramids of Egypt and the high-rise buildings of New York City. We even went up to the top of the Eiffel Tower after dark, the three of us hand in hand, silently viewing the lights of the city until the deafening sound of a jet plane roaring over-head broke the spell. That's when I found out that Barbra had just finished taking first-year French, and we start-ing pointing to every silly thing we saw and calling out *"Quel dommage!"* (What a pity!) until Andy threatened to strangle both of us unless we stopped, an ultimatum I quickly referred to as a *cri de coeur* — literally "a cry from the heart." Barbra latched on to that at once, pronounc-ing it over and over, until she got the tricky "cr" sound, with its distinctly French overtones, exactly right.

It was almost midnight when we finally made it to the Stratosphere, at the northern end of the Strip. We took the elevator all the way to the top for yet another absolutely breathtaking view of the entire city and miles beyond, illuminated by the light of the full moon shining down from above.

Fortunately for me, the thrill rides had closed down early that night, thus sparing me a near-certain heart attack should Barbra have wanted to be shot up an addi-tional 160 feet in the air and then dropped in free fall back down again — which, I'm sure, she would have.

Finally, to cap it all off, we stopped at the twenty-four-hour Denny's and ordered steak and eggs, hash browns, sliced tomatoes, rye toast, and black coffee. I'm not kidding when I tell you that it was more delicious than all the gourmet meals I've had in Paris put together.

We walked Barbra down the mostly deserted side streets until we arrived at the condo she shared with her father. She had to let herself in, since her father was not at home. "He's probably out on a date with Teri, his *regular* hound dog," she remarked, and then we all broke out into uncontrollable laughter. She promised to be ready to go at seven sharp in the morning, and that no, she *wouldn't* forget to bring the rocks. I had enough presence of mind to start back down the steps alone, leaving the two of them a moment in private to say good night. The slight pang I felt in my heart was bittersweet since it was nothing but a useless *cri de coeur,* leading to absolutely nowhere.

Andy and I walked a few blocks farther and caught the last bus of the night, heading for his own neighborhood, several miles on the other side of town. His mother was already asleep when we got there, so he quietly led me to the guest room with its adjoining bathroom. I noticed there was a little basket on the counter there with a selection of little bottles of lotion and shampoo and other personal amenities from a variety of motels and hotels. I poked around in there and saw that there were little soaps from places like the Pickwick Hotel in New York City, the Bartolomeo in Venice, and the Perak Lodge in Singapore. In answer to my quizzical look, Andy just shrugged and explained that his dad "traveled a lot on business." Then he pointed to a clock radio on the dresser and said that we'd have to leave about 6:45 in the morning and that maybe I should set it. And then he said that he'd be in the kitchen around 6:30 if I wanted to join him there for some cold cereal and juice.

"Okay. Thanks," I said. "And thanks again for letting me stay over. That's really nice of —"

"Sure. No problem." He was about to leave when he suddenly remembered something else. "Oh, I should tell you that there are probably a couple of cats sleeping under your bed — Sam and Spade, my father calls them. They are *really* in love with that wig you're wearing, so you'd better hang it up someplace where they can't get to it." He paused, and added with a little laugh, "I assume you *are* going to take it off? You seem to like it so much, I'm not sure."

"Oh, yeah," I assured him. "I'll take it off. But — uh, I was wondering, well, you're right, I do love it, and —"

"Hey, dude — say no more! It's yours!" He started to

leave again, but then he turned back and said quietly, as if to reassure me, "Don't worry, pal. Everything's going to be all right." He gave me the thumbs-up sign and shut the door.

Two seconds later he opened it again. "I almost forgot," he said. "No smoking. My mom will kill you."

"Oh." I nodded. "Okay."

"You really should quit, you know. It's bad for you."

Something about the way he said that brought a little ache right around my heart. *Does he really care that much about me?* "Yeah, well — I was thinking of doing that —"

"Good. See you in the morning then." And he closed the door again.

Before going to sleep, I spent almost a half hour trying to make contact with Angel Jake and the others in that mysterious and wholly spiritual world in that far-off other dimension that your science has yet to penetrate and — I'm sorry to report — never will.

I patiently explained to them how my human body was simply too bushed after such a long and eventful day to employ Protective Surveillance that night, since it required that I stay awake and alert, mentally on guard the entire time. Once I got their assurance that Barbra would survive the night in perfect safety, I allowed myself some intermittent moments of peaceful slumber, during which I dreamed of the two of us together, strolling hand in hand on the tiny Île Saint-Louis in the center of Paris, nibbling on ice-cream cones from Berthillon, the most renowned creamery in all the city, and surely the maker of the world's tiniest cones. We made them last as long as we could — those minuscule portions of ice cream perched atop our skinny cones — pointing them out to every tourist we passed, exclaiming, *"Quel dommage! Quel dommage!"* until the entire city finally slumbered under a blanket of sparkling stars that were no match for the magical beauty of the diamonds on her blouse. And last of all, just before I woke, there was the kiss. I shall hold it in my memory forever and ever, even throughout all eternity, and beyond.

chapter twenty

I WAS RUDELY AWAKENED the following morning by another communiqué from Up Above, in the usual form of a particularly severe blast to my head. It took me a few minutes to figure out what ol' Jake was trying to convey, but then it came to me in a flash. He was reminding me about that piece of folded paper that I had found stuck to the bottom of my rucksack at Angelo's — the piece of paper that I had just shoved into my pack without bothering to read.

Now I reached across the bed and retrieved it. I placed it on my nightstand and smoothed out the wrinkles as best I could with the side of my hand, trying not to notice how my fingers were trembling in nervous anticipation.

However, I soon discovered I had nothing to fear; it was merely a page torn out of the Office Furniture section of a store called Jack's Cut-Rate Furniture and Plumbing Supplies. The illustrations were clear enough, but I had to squint to read the printed material, since the ink was somewhat blurred and splotchy, which didn't surprise me in the least. This was a rather common occurrence with printed materials that arrived with me on my earthly assignments. (It probably has something to do with their highly unorthodox method of travel from the spiritual world to the physical, and the mingling of vastly different layers of ozone and other atmospheric variables. But I'm sure that you people would be able to explain that better than I ever could.)

It was right about then that the *strangest* thing happened. The room, which had been eerily quiet up until that time, was suddenly filled with "music" — for want of a better term. Startled, I momentarily forgot about the page from the catalog and glanced around the room, searching for some hidden speakers or, perhaps, a radio. Man, oh, man, did I feel stupid; of course, it was the clock radio that I had set the night before! A woman was singing in that loose and unrestrained screaming style that is so popular here on earth but *never* heard in Heaven. At first

the words were incomprehensible, but as she continued
her song, the lyrics became more and more distinct until I
was able to understand them completely:

> *The way back home is long and hard,*
> *And time, like magic, flies.*
> *But the way back home, the way back home*
> *Is right before your eyes.*

But here's the part that's *truly* strange: at the very
moment when she sang, "The way back home is right
before your eyes," my own eyes fell back on that page
from Jack's Cut-Rate Furniture catalog and on *one particular stool* that was very faintly circled in red. So you be
the judge. Was that a message, or was that a message? It
was a sleek-looking swivel stool with a pure white seat
perched atop a white pedestal, very distinct and modern
in style, and labeled the UPLIFTER. But can you imagine? A stool called the UPLIFTER? Only in WackiWorld!
But wait. There was an explanation. According to the page
of the catalog, the stool had a "special pneumatic feature
operated by an unseen button under the seat that would
raise the level of the stool to accommodate even the tallest
member of the family." The *UPLIFTER*? Of course! Ah —

but then it hit me like a bolt from the blue. How could I be so blind! What *else* could that be but a special message aimed directly at me! The UPLIFTER — destined to be my passport back to Paradise, lifting me up through the heights with grandeur and ease. Oh, Jakey boy, my eternal Best Buddy, you *are* the sly one, aren't you, pal?

Barbra was waiting for us on the steps leading up to her condo, just as we had planned. She was wearing a leopard-print blouse and tight blue jeans, with a white sweater draped over her arm. The same purse she had the day before was on her lap.

I was sitting in the front passenger seat in Andy's mother's Toyota as we drove up, but my signal for action came as soon as Barbra stood up and started walking toward the car.

Now picture this: I quickly hopped out and positioned myself behind the door, holding it wide open with my right hand placed confidently on the upper corner of the door frame. I smiled as she approached, and gently touched her right elbow with my free hand as I guided her into the front passenger seat that I had just vacated. When she was duly settled into position, I pulled up the metal portion of her seat belt and handed it to her, maintaining my gracious smile and bowing ever so slightly. Then I carefully shut her door firmly, but without undue force, and in one continuous movement, I slid nimbly into the backseat and closed the door behind me.

This entire procedure, when executed properly, is *de rigueur* for every well-bred Parisian youth in that ever-so-civilized city, and while Barbra didn't comment on my performance, I could tell by the look in her eyes and her murmured *"Merci, monsieur"* that she was genuinely impressed.

Andy, who was watching the whole thing, swiveled his head back into position and pulled away from the curb. "Got the rocks?" he asked, in what I thought was a slightly overly patronizing tone.

Apparently Barbra thought so as well. "No. I forgot them," she answered matter-of-factly.

"Good," he said.

She squirmed around a bit in her seat and then looked out the window. "Why do we have to be at the air-port so early? And I believe you're heading the wrong way, Andrew. The airport is *south* of my condo."

"No, sweetie, we're not going to McCarran. My uncle flies out of that little airport up in the north area — you know, off Rancho Drive?"

Come on, you two! Cut out the bickering! Andy, you can learn how to properly help a girl into a car! It's no big deal! And, Barbra, I'm sure you understand that he's feeling a twinge of jealousy right now. Go easy on him!

After a very tense moment, I saw Barbra slyly reach over and give his thigh a little squeeze. "Oh," she said simply. "I didn't know that." It wasn't exactly an apology, but it would do.

She let him drive in peace for a few minutes before she repeated her question. "So why *do* we have to be at the airport so early, anyway?"

How come we have to be there at all? That's what I'd like to know!

"Private pilots like to get an early start," Andy told her. "It has to do with the weather."

I cleared my throat as if I had something stuck in it, when all that I had stuck in it was pure, unadulterated fear. "Uh, Andy," I started, "how long has your uncle been flying, anyway?"

Barbra turned her head and looked at me. "Sounds like you're a little scared," she said, not at all sympathetic. "You only die once, you know."

Hey, not me, kiddo! I'm here forever! "Well, thanks a *lot*," I said to her. "That's a big comfort." I paused a moment, and then asked Andy again. "So, really, Andy — how long *has* he been flying? I'm just curious, that's all."

"Oh, for years and years. You don't have to worry about him. Believe me." And that's when I *really* began to worry.

Once we had arrived at the airport, Andy led us through the gate and out to the field itself, where several small planes were parked, all lined up in a neat row. His uncle was waiting for us there, whisk broom in hand, brushing off the backseats of a sparkling white Cessna.

"Well, this is it!" he said proudly as we approached. Then, all but ignoring us, he stepped back and gazed at the airplane as if he couldn't believe it himself. "My new little jewel!"

"Wow!" Andy said. "It's really something!" Then he put one arm around Barbra's shoulder and shook hands with his uncle. "These are the friends I told you about. Barbra DeMarco and Noah Sark."

"Happy to meet you," he said rather gruffly. "I see you're right on time. I like that."

"It's a pleasure to meet you, Mr. Bowman," Barbra said, surprising me by her sudden formality.

"Hey, cut out the Mister stuff," he replied, lightly

grasping her hand and shaking it almost limply, as if it might break. "Just call me Uncle Buck, same as this guy does," he added, giving Andy a light cuff on the chin.

Now it was my turn. "Glad to meet you, Uncle Buck," I said, taking his cue and cutting the Mister stuff.

"Right," he said, with a firm man-to-man shake.

He turned to Barbra. "So — you have the box?"

"The box?" she asked, looking up at *me*, as if I could help her.

"The ashes, honey. The remains. Andy said you wanted to drop some ashes, so —"

"Oh, no," Andy corrected. "Not ashes —"

"Just these rocks," Barbra said, pulling the little plastic bag out of her purse. "Just these."

Uncle Buck took the bag out of her hand. "You want to drop these? What the Hell for?" He paused and inspected them a little more closely. "What's so special about them? They look like ordinary rocks to me."

Barbra got this sort of helpless look on her face. "It's kind of a long story. See, I —"

"It's just a personal thing," Andy broke in. "Nothing important. Well, maybe important to *her*, but not to anyone else."

That seemed good enough for Uncle Buck, who was

now really giving Barbra the once-over. "You sure remind me of somebody," he said, shifting his eyes over to Andy. "Who does she remind me of?"

Andy didn't seem to want to go there. He just looked at her and shrugged. "I don't know. Who?"

I couldn't bear to see Barbra's bright smile replaced by pouting lips and reproachful eyes, so I took over. "Princess Diana, maybe?" I suggested. "Some people think —"

Uncle Buck snapped his fingers. "That's it. Princess Diana."

Barbra immediately stuck her tongue out at Andy for about a tenth of a second. It was *so* like her! And *so* cute!

"And as for you, son," Uncle Buck was saying, looking at my hair, "I recognize *part* of you, that's for sure." He laughed a no-nonsense kind of laugh and kind of slicked down the hair on the side of his head.

Now he looked at Andy. "So your dad's retiring that one, huh? Man, oh, man, if wigs could only talk." He clasped his hands behind his back and glanced up at the sky. "Well, weather still looks good. I guess I'm ready to go, if you are." He leaned toward Andy, lowered his voice a little, and took on a tone of confidentiality. "And that other thing, is that all settled —"

Andy grabbed him by the arm and gave it a squeeze.

"Oh," Uncle Buck responded with a nod. He took out his wallet and poked around in it for a moment before extracting a couple of one-dollar bills, which he handed to me. "Noah, do me a favor, will you? If you pass through that gate behind you there, and go straight into the building, you'll see some stairs leading up to the coffee shop. Bring me back a large black coffee, please," he said, "and keep the change."

He nodded at Barbra. "And you go with him. But listen, *don't* bring anything back for yourselves, y'hear? I've got a brand-new airplane there, and I don't want any spills."

While we were waiting for the coffee, Barbra suddenly said something to me that almost made me fall down in a faint. "You want to hear something funny?" she asked.

"Sure. What?"

"I just wanted to tell you, I dreamed about you last night. We were in Paris."

That was it. That was all. The server pressed a lid onto the coffee cup and set it down. "Anything else?" she asked.

Barbra looked at me. I was unable to speak. "No, just

coffee," she answered. Then she took the bills from my hand and handed them to the woman.

"Come on," she said. "Let's go. They're waiting for us down on the field."

"Uh, something's come up, kids," Uncle Buck said as Barbra handed him the cup of coffee. "It looks like we'll have to make a little detour over to the Calaveras County Airport after we do the drop-off in Death Valley."

He glanced at Andy before continuing. "A friend of mine up there is having a little trouble with his transponder and wants to borrow my old one." He paused a moment and cleared his throat, swirling his coffee around in the cup.

"Anyway, young lady," he continued, looking at Barbra now, "I thought I'd better let you know, in case you need to check with your —"

"Oh, that's okay!" she broke in. "We're in no hurry to get back. In fact, this is even better! Now we'll get a longer ride!" She looked at me. "Right?"

She dreamed about me! She actually dreamed *about me!* I nodded, still in a daze. "Right."

"Well, hop in then," said the pilot. "Here, Barbra — you sit up in front, next to me. That window opens, so you'll be able to do the tossing. But *not* until I give the word!"

"Oh, this is so cool!" she exclaimed. "I can't believe it's actually happening!"

In a few minutes we were all settled in the cockpit, snug as bugs in a rug. Uncle Buck gave us our final instructions. "Are you all seat-belted? Good. Now you'll notice that you all have headsets there, but I'd prefer that you didn't use them. All you'd hear is a bunch of pilot jabber, and I don't encourage cockpit chatter. It only serves to distract the pilot, especially old farts like me. But what you *could* do is keep your eyes peeled for other aircraft in the vicinity. Just give me a holler if they appear to be too close for comfort."

I turned to Andy, sitting there beside me. "Is he *kidding*?" I said quite loudly, since the engine was firing up. "Doesn't he have *radar* or something?"

Andy shrugged. "I don't know. He always tells me to watch for other aircraft whenever I go up with him, so I don't think he's kidding."

Well, that's just ducky! And by the way, where are our parachutes, for pity's sake?

"Here we go, folks," Uncle Buck announced. "Hold on to your hats. Up, up, and awaaay."

I think I must have been in my serious prayer mode all the way to Death Valley, because before I knew it, Uncle Buck was pointing to the barren ground below and shouting in Barbra's ear. "That's it! We're flying over the Monument now. So just pick out a spot and I'll bank a bit and you can make the drop."

Everything went pretty well, except that when Barbra opened her window, the sudden rush of air just grabbed that bag right out of her hand — before she had a chance to remove the rocks — and the whole thing went flying off into the blue. She was okay with it, though. And I must say that she actually did seem a lot more carefree — or perhaps *unburdened* would be a better word — after the deed was done.

Who knows? I wondered. *Perhaps Gloria-Marie and some of those psychics are not so Evil after all, if they can actually be of help to people with problems such as Barbra's.*

Oh, Lordy-*Lord*! Did I get a head whopping after *that* thought crossed my mind! I instantly recognized it for what it was — a timely warning from Up Above about the powers of Satan, The Evil One, who is forever on the watch for the slightest chink in the armor of the righteous. Was I just a bit too cocky, tempting the Great

Tempter and forgetting my superiors' constant reminder that Satan was once an Angel himself? Apparently so!

But still, in my own defense, it was only a *thought*, after all! Oh, I know from experience that certain members of my Heavenly superiors can be unreasonable on occasion, and sometimes punitive and given to outrageous tests of loyalty, but simple pettiness? Was that ever in the mix? Well, come to think of it, I suppose it was — but only now and then.

CHAPTER TWENTY-ONE

I HAD NO IDEA THAT the Calaveras County Airport was just seven miles away from Angels Camp until I happened to notice the large map on the wall in the airport terminal. I mean, how *could* I know an obscure thing like that? I was about to fault Angel Jake again for not supplying me with that important info, until I realized that he actually *did*, by directing my path right in front of the map. *Sorry, Angel Jake. I was too quick to judge.*

Andy came over then and suggested that we hitch a ride into town while his uncle was meeting with his friend. "Hey," he said brightly, "maybe we could surprise your parents and just show up at your house!"

"Oh, darn!" I replied. "They're out of town. They

always go to, uh — Acapulco around this time of year. A time-share thing, you know." *Talk about being on my toes! I rate at least an A-minus for that show of extemporaneous originality.*

Andy didn't seem surprised to hear that. "Oh, that's too bad," he said. "But let's at least go into town and get a bite to eat or something." He paused. "My uncle recommended a great little deli on Main Street."

Barbra agreed. "Good idea. But how will we get over there? This map shows that it's too far to walk to from here."

"Well, my uncle told me that you can usually find guys hanging around the terminal here that are available for hire. The only thing is, they're not licensed or anything, so you have to be on your toes when you bargain with them."

Barbra looked a bit doubtful. "Why don't we just call a cab?"

"In this burg? Are you kidding?"

"Well, actually," she said, "I don't think it's a very good idea to just hitch a ride with some stranger —"

My feelings exactly! "Why don't we ask that airport person over there?" I suggested. "See her there, behind the desk? She should know who the regulars are around here."

"Good idea," Barbra said. "I'll go check with her."

Andy and I watched as she and the woman had a short conversation. Then she signaled for us to follow her out the front door. She pointed to this guy leaning against the building smoking a cigarette.

"He's okay," she said. "His name is Henri."

Henri! No! Never! I thought my head was going to split open, the pain was so bad. In fact, I thought I should sit down before I fell down, but there was no place to sit except right on the cement, and I didn't want to do that. So I just put my palms against my forehead and gripped the top of my head and pressed down as hard as I could. I shut my eyes for a second, but that made me so dizzy that I quickly opened them again.

Barbra had spoken to the man by then and had walked back over to us. "The guy says he'll do it for twenty bucks, including a tip," reported Barbra. "I say let's go for it."

"No!" I shouted out. *"Not him!"*

She and Andy were so startled that they both backed away from me a couple of steps. "Jesus!" Andy exclaimed. "Calm down, okay? What's wrong, buddy?"

I took a deep breath. My head felt much better now. "Anybody but *that* guy," I said steadily. "Anybody but him."

Andy and Barbra just looked at each other, tightening the muscles around their jaws and mouths, making faces that expressed their disbelief much better than words. Barbra started to dispute me, though. "Well, what's *wrong* with him —" she started to say.

But Andy shushed her and stood up for me. "It doesn't matter," he said. Then he indicated a woman sitting on a bench a short distance away. "What about her, Noah? How does she look?" I was really touched by the sudden, quiet concern I heard in his voice.

I nodded. "She's okay."

Barbra agreed. "Yeah, she's all right."

We all walked over to the lady on the bench, leaving Barbra to ask the questions. The woman quickly agreed to take us to town for fifteen dollars, but first, she said, she wanted to use the restroom. We all agreed that was a good idea. When we finally piled into her car, I noticed that Henri was no longer there.

We saw him a few minutes later, though — and it was terrible — so *terrible*! His car was overturned in the ditch by the side of the road, and six or seven cyclists were swarming around it. One guy was on the phone, and a couple of the others were struggling to pull poor Henri out of the mangled vehicle, and there was blood all around. Our driver lady slowed down as we passed, just as the car in the ditch burst into flame.

"God! Oh, God!" Barbra screamed, covering her eyes. "Thank goodness they got him out in time!"

Our driver stepped on the gas then. "They don't need us here," she remarked. "I'm sure help is on the way."

A minute later, Barbra, who was sitting in the front seat, turned around and looked me straight in the eye. "You saved our lives," she said simply. "Maybe you really *are* my Guardian Angel."

Well, that's it. That's what I've been waiting for. The signs are so obvious, it can't be anything else. I actually saved her life! She even said so herself! The driver's name was Henri. That was no mere coincidence! Oh, Hallelujah! I passed the test! What a relief! But just to be sure, to be doubly sure, I'll bide my time for a while longer. Just to be sure. There may be other signs. Just to be sure.

No one spoke until the lady pulled into a parking space on Main Street, in the center of town. "How's this?" she asked. "Shall I let you off here?"

Andy was straining to see out the front window. "Is there a deli along here somewhere? My uncle mentioned a deli."

"Oh, yes," she said, pulling out of the parking place. "It's up this next block."

A minute later she was parking the car a few doors past the deli.

"This is perfect," said Andy, looking first at Barbra and then at me, and then finally reaching for his wallet.

"Hey, let me get this," I said, thinking about all those twenties about to go to waste.

Andy shrugged. "Well, if you insist."

"Thanks, Noah," Barbra said, opening her door. "That's really nice of you."

"My pleasure."

I gave the lady a twenty and told her to keep the change.

"When are we supposed to be back at the airport?" Barbra asked as we entered the deli.

Andy was holding the door open. "Oh, it'll be an hour or two, at least. Uncle Buck said he'd call me. He said he'd meet us here at the deli." He paused a moment, then added something to the effect that maybe Uncle Buck was going to bring some "friends" back here with him. There was something about the studied nonchalance in his tone that made me feel kind of curious — kind of edgy, in fact. "Friends?" I inquired. "What kind of friends?"

But Andy just shrugged and let the door swing shut and then headed toward a cluster of unoccupied tables.

Meanwhile, Barbra had stopped to examine the little toys in the dispensing machines standing next to the cash register. "Oh, look!" she said, stooping down to get a better view. "Look at those little purple slimy things, and those cute little Angel key rings. Aren't they cute, Andy?"

But Andy had found us a table by then and was already sitting down.

"Which one do you like?" I asked, reaching into my pocket. "The Angel key rings, or those little purple slimy things?"

Oh, the sweet, sweet pain of it all! If I can just buy her a little Angel key ring, at least she'd have something to remember me by. Maybe when she gets her own house and her own car, she'll really use that key chain and handle it every day! Maybe she'll keep it forever — and, someday, when she becomes an old lady and can no longer get around, she'll still look at it occasionally, and think of me —

"*You* decide," she said with a laugh.

"That's easy." I put four quarters in the machine and

turned the little handle, while Barbra bent down and lifted the metal lid right under it to claim her prize.

"It's sweet," she said, delicately holding up the tiny Angel by its little chain. "It's sweet," she repeated. "Just like you."

If there are words to express how I felt at that moment, I've never heard them — not on earth, and not in Heaven.

A few minutes later, after we were all sitting down and had placed our orders, I spotted Angelo on the television, just as I related to you earlier. Some crazy tourist who remembered Angelo back in the days when he played Sergio the Singing Waiter on that TV show began taunting him with the forbidden "Ka-*Boom*sy" routine, and Angelo just went berserk. Pandemonium followed. The *Noon News* crew showed up even before the police, and when the camera panned around in back of the counter over by the cold-drinks refrigerator case, there was that strangely beautiful stool, calling out to me, *The way back home, the way back home.* And from that moment on, there was no longer any doubt in my mind. Ready or not, it was time for me to go.

When I went to the john a little while later, intending to escape through the window, an employee of the deli was in there fiddling around with the hand dryer.

I was disappointed that there was no window in the room through which I might have made my getaway. But then, even if there *had* been a window, I still wouldn't have been able to make my escape, with that guy in the room.

"What happened? That thing not working?" I asked as I was rinsing my hands in the sink.

"Worse than that," he said, looking up. "It's completely busted. There was a Helluva ruckus here on Friday afternoon — a bunch of high-school kids horsing around on the last day of school. It had something to do with a pet frog. One of the guys made a lunge for it and cracked his head on the dryer here."

I knew it! Didn't I say those things were dangerous? Was I right, or was I right?

"I happened to see him leaving. He was really out of it, wobbling around like a prizefighter about to go down for the count."

"Hmm. No kidding." Actually, I wasn't paying much attention to the guy. I was trying to think of another way of escaping from Barbra and Andy and getting back to

Angelo's and that magical UPLIFTER stool as fast as I could.

"I feel bad now that I didn't stop him."

"Who?"

"That kid. The one I'm telling you about. I saw him get in his car and take off, and I should have stopped him. The thing is, the guy kind of disappeared after that. He was a good kid, too. *Is* a good kid, I should say, because he must be around somewhere. Really smart, too, and what an imagination! He actually spent last summer in Europe on one of those Hands Across the Sea programs or some damn thing affiliated with his church."

"Hmm," I said, busy examining myself in the mirror. I was surprised to see that I had started to grow a beard. Well, not a beard, exactly. A five-o'clock shadow, at least. Maybe even six o'clock. With that, along with my wig, I hardly recognized myself.

"Naturally, his parents are frantic," the repairman was saying. "I sure hope he turns up soon."

"Yeah. I hope so, too," I said, pushing the door open. I didn't mean to be rude, but I couldn't waste any more time listening to him when I should have been thinking about how I might make my escape.

*   *   *

Well, here I am, still on the Greyhound. The driver is announcing that we'll be in Las Vegas in ten minutes, so we should start gathering up all our stuff. I just have my rucksack, so I'm okay.

I can't help thinking about the lady who picked me up across the street from the drugstore in Angels Camp (where I was supposed to be buying a pack of cigarettes!) and brought me to Modesto, where I caught this bus. I didn't even go into the drugstore, but just asked a woman standing on the sidewalk there where I could get a bus to Las Vegas, and she said I should go to Modesto. So I crossed over to the other side of Main Street and stood there with my thumb out, and this nice old lady in a big, fancy Mercedes stopped right on the street, not seeming to mind that she was double-parked and holding up traffic. She rolled down her window, and I stuck my head in and said, "I need a lift to Modesto. Are you going that way?"

She immediately unlocked the door from her side and motioned for me to get in. I opened the door, put my rucksack down on the floor mat, and climbed in.

"I really appreciate —" I started to say, but she interrupted me.

"I've been expecting you," she said, with the sweetest little twinkle in her eyes.

I was a little taken aback, of course. "Really? Well —"

"You see, my husband passed away last Tuesday, and I've been waiting for you." She managed to keep her eyes on the road all the time she was talking. Actually, it was kind of creepy, in a way. "I just *knew* the Lord would help me through these difficult days, and now here you are!"

Her face broke into a slow, gentle smile, but she still didn't look at me. "And when I drop you off in Modesto, I know that I shall never see you again. But I won't need to. You'll be in my heart forever, for you are truly my Guardian Angel."

I felt no connection with her in the least, and I knew she couldn't be more mistaken. I also knew that without my Angel curls, she would never have given me a second glance.

According to my sacred Angel Code, I couldn't let her mistaken belief go unchallenged. "I am deeply touched by your faith," I said as gently as I could. "But I must tell you — I am not *your* Guardian Angel."

For the first time, she turned to look at me, her whole face transfixed with a Heavenly glow. "Hush," she whispered. "I know what I know, and nothing that you can say will ever change that."

She stopped the car in front of the bus station, but she didn't turn off the engine. She just reached out one hand and very lovingly touched my cheek and then, very briefly, my beautiful golden curls. "Good-bye," she whispered. "And thank you so much for coming."

What a true denizen of your planet! A delusional dreamer wandering aimlessly in WackiWorld, ready and willing to believe anything that offers comfort, peace of mind, and the promise of immortality. And that, of course, is why I am here.

At last I arrive back in Las Vegas. In spite of the lateness of the hour, the streets are not yet deserted. I see the lights of the Stratosphere shining like a beacon, directing me to my final destination.

There are very few customers at Angelo's now. I enter slowly, my all-too-human heart pounding rapidly in my chest. The nighttime clerk is not behind the counter, but I soon spot him sitting at one of the tables, his head buried in his arms and a lighted cigarette dangling from his fingers. Like a thief in the night, I very quietly make my way unnoticed behind the counter. And there it is, my pure white UPLIFTER in all its glory, waiting for me in front of the cold-drinks refrigerator case. With a prayer on my lips and a heart overflowing with love for all the people on earth, I lower myself onto its velvety-cushioned seat, close my eyes, and wait.